PIECE OF *Me*

BEHIND THESE EYES BOOK 2

A.J. DANIELS

NOTE FROM THE AUTHOR

The author has taken creative liberties with all names, places, and organizations mentioned in this book, and are not a reflection of any person, living or dead, or organization.

Piece of Me is the second book in the Behind These Eyes series but each book in the series can be read as a standalone, although, it's recommended to read them in order. Make sure you stick around for an **unedited** excerpt of *Always You* at the back of the book

PROLOGUE
Katherine

The thing about love is that you don't get to choose who you fall in love with or when you fall in love. Most of the time you never see it coming.

Then there are those times when you see it coming, and even though you try everything in your power to prevent it from happening it still smacks into you like a semi-truck. Just like the way I fell in love with Jason. He was my best friend. My protector. I was perfectly happy with our relationship the way it was. As friends. Until I wasn't.

I was about to learn that sometimes the person you don't want to love is the one you end up falling for the most.

And I fell hard.

1. TEQUILA

Katherine

Some loud obnoxious beeping rouses me from a very enticing dream. Hugh Jackman is doing really, *really* delicious things with his tongue and I don't want him to stop.

Damn, that man is talented.

When he lifts his head, I'm expecting that sexy Australian accent to do me in, but all that comes out when his lips move is that annoying beep.

Frustrated, I throw my arm out in the general direction of my night stand but instead of hitting solid wood, my arm connects with solid muscle and a huff sounds from my right.

The events of last night flash in my mind's eye like a stop motion movie. The six of us at the bar. Shots of tequila. *Lots* of tequila. Dancing by myself. Jay dancing with me. There was kissing. Lots of kissing, and lots of…touching.

I sit bolt upright suddenly realizing that I'm naked and the solid wall of muscle my arm just hit belongs to Jay.

Oh, fuck my life!

I run a hand down my face in horror. I can't believe I slept with Jason. Sure, we've been flirting back and forth for over a year now but it was never meant to go beyond that. It was never meant to get physical. This is why I'm not allowed around tequila. It makes me do horribly stupid things that I would never do when I'm sober.

I peek out of my right eye and am met by a set of very drool-worthy abs.

Holy shit, the guy has the body of a Greek god.

A trail of golden hair leads down to that 'v' muscle I love so much on guys, but I'm slightly disappointed when the lower half of his body is covered by my navy-blue duvet cover.

A slight chuckle snaps my attention away from that muscle and to his face. God, this man is beautiful. Square jaw with light stubble, straight nose, and amazing emerald eyes that are staring back at me. A smirk pulling at his lips. A lock of dark blond hair hangs down his forehead.

"Like what you see?" he teases.

I roll my eyes. "Don't look so pleased with yourself. Tequila was involved."

I gather the sheet closer around my body and move towards the bathroom.

He laughs. "You can keep denying it, but this was bound to happen. And I wouldn't say no to another round...or two." He shoots me a wink when I poke my head out from the bathroom.

"Were you always this cocky?"

He grins. "Not cocky, babe. Confident."

I snort and roll my eyes turning back to start the shower. "Yeah, well, I'm confident that this will never happen again." I call from the bathroom.

"You sure about that?" he says startling me when he suddenly appears in the doorway.

"Seriously? Why do you have to sneak up on me like that." I grip the sheet tighter.

This man has the power to undo me and I'm not totally sure that I'm okay with it. I like being in control, in all aspects. It was the reason for almost every one of my breakups and why I'm currently single. Men just don't like a woman who loves being in control.

But it was the one thing that I didn't think I would be able to give up. Being in control kept my anxiety at bay and I didn't like the way I felt when I was anxious.

I flake out of a lot of things when my anxiety runs rampant. I somehow manage to talk myself out of leaving my house and just staying curled up under my duvet cover watching Netflix. Even something as simple as going to the grocery store becomes a nightmare. I've quit many a job because of anxiety.

But this man standing in front of me, gloriously naked, is threatening to undo that control.

He cups my face with his hand and his thumb runs gently up

and down my cheek bone, his emerald eyes staring intently into my amber ones.

"Stop fighting it," he whispers.

"I can't." I drop my head causing his hand to fall away from my face.

I miss his touch instantly. *I wish I was normal.* I wish I could stay wrapped up in him. But I can't and I doubt I'll ever be able to.

He hangs his head and takes a step back. I want to reach out to him to stop him from leaving but my arms don't move and nothing comes out when I open my mouth.

"I'll see you around, Kat."

I'm not sure how long I stand there staring out the doorway to my room. I don't even remember Jay getting dressed or hearing the front door open and close. But when I finally get into the shower the water is like ice.

Jason

"You look like someone just shot your dog," Mike calls from the boxing ring when I walk through the gym door.

"Long night," I throw over my shoulder, placing my gym bag on the bench and grabbing my boxing gloves and wraps from it.

"I bet," Mike laughs. "So, how was it?"

I know he's talking about Kat. It's been a long running joke in our circle of friends that we should just fuck and get it over with. Apparently, the sexual tension when we're around each other is noticeable to everyone in a fifty-mile radius.

I love Mike like a brother but right now I want to punch his fucking face in for that comment. It usually wouldn't bother me this much but I was already in a bad mood after leaving Kat's.

Fuck, I get it. She's scared. None of her asshole exes stuck around for very long but they were weak. They didn't appreciate what they had in front of them. If it came down to it, I would take a bullet for that woman.

And that right there, ladies and gentlemen, is why I'm in a pissed off mood. This woman can frustrate me and make me the happiest I've ever been in the span of a few minutes. She's constantly testing my limits, making me work harder than any other woman has before.

But when she laughs, it's the most beautiful sound I've ever heard and I forget about how difficult and frustrating she can be. And when she cries, I want to protect her from the world and hunt down the person responsible and make them pay for every single one of her tears.

She'll never see me as anything other than the party boy though. The king of one-night stands. Even though Mike takes the cake for that last one.

I'll only ever be her best guy friend who she just happened to sleep with after a night of one too many tequila shots. A half smile pulls at the corner of my mouth. *But what a fucking great night it was.*

"You okay, man?" Parker asks sitting on the bench next to me and my grin fades.

I don't take my eyes off Mike sparring with Cole in the ring. "I'm good. Just need to go a few rounds in the ring,"

Out of the corner of my eye I see Parker stand, picking up his gym bag. "Dani and Bell are cooking dinner tonight."

Dani started letting Bella help her in the kitchen when she went to live with them permanently. Bella was so excited the first time she was able to help that she begged Parker to invite us all over for dinner that night.

After that, it's been an unspoken tradition that if Bella's helping with dinner, all of us are invited.

"I'll be there."

The sound of laughter greets me as I walk into Parker's house this evening. I follow it to the kitchen where Bella is standing on a step stool grating cheese next to Dani. Kat and Alice are sitting on the other side of the center island with half-filled glasses of white wine. After the situation with Adam ended, Dani decided to not go back to her previous identity as Ashley Martens; however, Kat and Alice decided they wanted to go back to their original identities. To who they were before Adam threatened all their lives.

Kat doesn't see me at first, which allows me a second to stare at her. Not in a fucking creepy way. But how can you see someone as beautiful as she is and not stare?

The sun streaming in from the kitchen window accentuates the subtle red highlights in her long, curly, dark hair. I remember the way it felt running through my fingers; it was like silk. Her perfectly round ass is perched high on a bar stool. Her amber eyes sparkling with amusement at something Bella has just done.

This woman is beauty personified. Not just physical beauty either. She's beautiful on the inside too.

We met two and a half years ago, when Dani and Parker had first started seeing each other. In those short couple years, I've seen her go toe-to-toe with someone double her size because they were harassing a homeless man. I've watched her give that same homeless man the last bit of change she had, even knowing that he would probably turn around and use it towards buying more booze or drugs.

I've watched her cry during movies but try to cover it up before anyone could notice. I've seen the way her eyes light up when we walk past a pet store and she sees all the puppies in the window but then in the next second she's angry because they probably came from a puppy mill.

But she'll never know how I feel because she's determined to firmly place the 'just friends' label on us.

Fuck. I need to grow some balls and get over it.

"Oh hey, Jay. Parker and Mike are in the den watching the game," Danielle says when she spins around and sees me standing in the entrance to the kitchen.

I don't chance another glance over at Kat before I turn and head down the hallway.

I remember the day she first confided in me about what she was passionate about. We had been on our first vacation as a group and Kat and I had gone off to walk along one of the side streets off the main drag.

~ Two, almost three, months ago, June. ~

"Kat!" I yell after her when she suddenly stops, turns, and takes off back the way we came. It takes me a minute to realize that she's running straight to a little cove surrounded on either side by cliffs. Then I hear it.

It's faint at first but the more I concentrate on the sound, the louder it becomes. As the cove and Kat come more into view my feet slow and my heart rate picks up.

I can barely make out their silhouettes in the dark but trapped in the cove is a pod of bottlenose dolphins; adults and babies.

I get the eerie feeling that we're not supposed to be here. Someone went through an awful lot of trouble to do everything they could to block this cove off from prying eyes. From the high fence to the signs. I can't read them because they're not in English, but if I had to guess, I'd guess they said something along the lines of *Do Not Enter*.

But Kat doesn't stop, she's already climbing the fence and dropping to her feet on the other side before kicking off her shoes and running into the water.

"Jesus, Kat!"

"Help me, Jay," she throws over her shoulder when she's already waist deep in the water.

Christ, this woman's going to be the death of me.

Scaling the ten-foot high fence, my boots hit the sand on the other side seconds before I'm running down the beach and into the water after her.

"We need to cut the net," she yells as she bobs up and down in the freezing water.

I pat down the pockets of my jeans in search of the utility knife I always carry with me. *Old habits die hard, I guess.* As soon as I pull the knife into my palm I swim over to the net and start cutting through several of the ropes.

A flash of light to our right towards the shore catches my attention, my hands work faster trying to cut through the rope and once the final one snaps I'm hauling ass back to Kat, grabbing her arm and pulling her to the side and behind a bunch of tall rocks just as we hear the click of a lock and the fence rolling open.

"What's going on?" one voice asks sounding further away.

"I don't know. I thought I saw something in the water by the net," a voice closer to the shore yells back in broken English.

"It's just those damn dolphins! The trainers will be here tomorrow," the first voice calls back.

"Jason," Kat whispers in front of me.

"Shh." I try to peek behind her and around the rock to see where the two men have gone but she tugs on my arm drawing my attention back to her. It's dark and I can just barely make her out against the black of the rocks.

"My shoes."

"What?"

"I kicked my shoes off on the sand just before running into the water."

"Maybe they won't- "

As soon as the words leave my lips a spotlight gets turned on and more voices are yelling from the beach.

Fuck!

"Go," I push her in front of me and up the rocky embankment to the tree line.

Voices yell behind us to stop but our legs keep propelling us forward until we break out of the tree line and onto the boardwalk. Running feet get closer as my eyes scan the crowd and the buildings.

I'm pulling her through the front doors of a nearby café and towards the back by the counter, angling our bodies away from the café's front windows, just as the men break the tree line.

The barista behind the counter is eyeing us up and down. The whole thing would've been comical if we hadn't just been illegally trespassing and weren't soaking wet.

Kat looks at the barista, shrugs her shoulders and just casually says, "what's a vacation without a spontaneous night swim," then giggles and turns back towards the door, coffee in hand.

After I make sure that we're not being chased anymore, we grab a pair of flip flops for her, and I slow down our pace as we make our way back to the resort.

"Okay, now would you mind telling me what that was about?"

She sighs, outlining the lid of her coffee cup with a finger. "Every year twenty-three thousand dolphins are slaughtered in that cove. Those are just the ones that aren't chosen by trainers for a life of captivity. I didn't know that they would have any dolphins in there now. The season was supposed to be over two months ago, in March."

Tears are flowing down her face as we near the entrance to our resort and she stops walking. "When I heard them crying I had to be sure that I wasn't imagining the sound. And then when I saw that they had trapped babies as well I knew I couldn't just let them be killed. They don't take the babies, Jason. They poke and prod them and let them bleed out until they sink to the bottom. I just…I couldn't…"

"Shh, it's okay, Kat. I get it." I wrap my arms around her and hold her until the tears subside.

"How can humans be so cruel? What makes one life more worthwhile than another? And since when did education become about sticking a living breathing thing behind bars or in a tiny pool behind a glass? It's bullshit, Jason. They wouldn't be allowed to slaughter these animals if people would stop visiting those stupid aquariums or swim-with programs." Kat pulls away from my arms and turns her back on me so that I won't see her crying.

"I'm not following. How does what they do here relate to aquariums?"

Her shoulders rise and fall with each breath. "Those fishermen drive thousands of dolphins a year into that cove and then trainers from aquariums, hotels, and swim-with-dolphin programs from around the world come down and pay tens-of-thousands of dollars for the young female bottlenoses and the rest they…" She inhales deeply, spinning on her heels to face me. "The rest they slaughter and sell labelled as other meat."

Kat shakes her head, her sad eyes looking up at me. "Dolphin meat is extremely high in mercury and those people don't even know that the meat they're buying could kill them."

"Jesus."

"I wish I could do more. This needs to stop. It's barbaric and if they keep slaughtering those dolphins they could go extinct in our lifetime, Jason." She shakes her head in disbelief. "In our lifetime," she repeats. Her shoulders drop in defeat. "But I'm just one person. There's no way I would even be able to put a dent in dolphin slaughter."

"It only takes one voice."

"Easier said than done."

Kat huffs, crossing her arms over her chest. I hate seeing her this hurt. Her heart is breaking for those dolphins we let free from the nets enclosing them in that cove. But her heart isn't just breaking for them but for all the others before them and the ones that will be driven in after them.

I have never wished more that I could put a stop to the evil in this world the way I did that day, hearing her talk about those dolphins.

2. NOT SUPPOSED TO LOVE YOU

Katherine

"Wow, awkward much?" Alice comments next to me.

"You can say that again," I whisper.

I feel like a grade-A bitch for not even acknowledging Jason when he entered the kitchen. I knew he was there the minute he turned the corner. I could feel his eyes on me but I chose to ignore it. To ignore him.

I just wasn't ready to deal with the aftermath of last night and waking up to find him butt naked in my bed this morning.

"Can we just change the subject, please?" I beg.

"How's the new job going?" Dani asks over her shoulder while she helps Bella stir the chili.

I shrug. "So far, so good. I haven't met my boss yet."

"Aren't you the assistant to the CEO?" Alice asks.

I nod. "I am, but he's been away on a business trip this entire week. I'll probably get to meet him next week when he gets back."

"Aunty Kat, will you come to my game?" Bella asks, climbing down from her step stool.

Danielle laughs. "They finally have their first game this weekend and Bell just made defense. I don't think I've ever seen Parker as happy as he was when she told him she wanted to play soccer this summer and hockey in the winter."

"Will you come, Aunty Kat? Please? Aunt Alice already said she would come," Bella pleads next to me.

"Sure thing, Princess. I'll be there," I smile down at her.

Her excitement is radiating off her in waves. I don't think I've seen Bella this happy or excited about something since Danielle and Parker's wedding several months ago.

"Yay! I'm going to go tell Dad that you're coming," Bella yells, turning on her heels and racing down the hallway.

"Some days that kid makes me feel old," Danielle shakes her head. "I wish I had half her energy."

"Just wait until she turns sixteen or starts dating," Alice teases.

Danielle groans. "Parker's already said she's not allowed to date until she's thirty. I swear he's building his gun collection just for the day she brings home a boy."

"I feel sorry for the poor bastard. He'll have not one but three over-protective males to get through before he can take that girl on a date," Alice adds and the three of us laugh at the thought of Parker, Jason, and Mike standing in a protective line between Bella and her date. Think Will Smith and Martin Lawrence in *Bad Boys II* but bigger and scarier.

"So, what kind of company are you working for, Kat? I feel like I've been out of the loop with Bell's adoption and then the wedding," Danielle says over her shoulder while taking down plates to set the table.

"It's an advertising company but they also own a whole bunch of media outlets like a local TV station, newspapers, and magazines."

"According to every article ever written about the CEO, David Walker, he felt that local artists and business weren't getting the recognition they deserved and he didn't want to see them being eaten up by big corporations, so he built Walker Advertising from the ground up starting when he was twenty-two and fresh out of university," Alice adds.

"He has his hand in a variety of other companies as well. The advertising firm is just one under the Walker umbrella."

"Well, I'm happy for you, Kat."

"Thanks, D. This job will definitely get me that much closer to my dream job. This was the foot in the door that I needed."

After we've set the table, Dani pokes her head around the corner to the hallway and calls, "dinner's ready!"

As always, I'm running early and nobody is at the rec centre yet for Bella's soccer game. So, while I wait for the rest of the group to get here, I crank up the A/C in my car and lean my seat back a little, getting lost in the voices of Lee Brice and Chris Young. I may have been raised in the city all my life but I'm not your typical city girl. I love country music, spending hours at the range, going 4x4-ing, and I'm not completely opposed to going hunting one day. I'm not afraid to get dirty and I practically live in jeans and tank tops. Alice is constantly chastising me about my wardrobe but I can't help that I think wearing dresses and skirts is dreadfully uncomfortable. It used to drive my mother nuts too. But everything about me used to drive my mother nuts, even my existence.

A loud rap on my passenger window causes my heart to jump up my throat. When I look over, Jay's wearing a shit-eating grin. My first thought was to just leave him out there but then my eyes fall and landed on two venti sized coffee cups. That is the only reason I find myself pressing the button to unlock the passenger door for him.

"You've got to stop sneaking up on me like that," I huff while he settles himself into the seat of my Honda Civic.

Jay doesn't say anything just laughs and hands me one of the cups before reaching over and turning down the A/C. I shoot him my best impression of a death glare as he turns it all the way down. I love the summer and the heat but it's currently forty degrees Celsius outside and heading towards the end of August.

The smooth taste of espresso, steamed milk, and extra caramel syrup makes me sigh in contentment.

"You're forgiven," I tell him before taking another sip of the heavenly drink.

He chuckles, "I should be for what that drink costs."

"Hey, no talking smack about the drink of the gods."

He holds up both hands, one palm out facing me, the other

holding onto his own coffee cup. "Won't happen again," he teases.

"How'd you know I would be here already anyway?"

He smirks. "You've always been early to everything ever since I met you. I think it's physically impossible for you to be late, Kat."

He's got a point. My anxiety is a contradictory bitch. On one hand, it takes me forever to talk myself into leaving my apartment but then it also never allows me to be late. The thought of being late makes me sick to my stomach. In university, if I knew that I was going to be late getting to a class, I just wouldn't go. There's nothing worse than walking in late to a lecture with a hundred other students and have everyone turn to look at you as the door creaks closed behind you. Why are the doors to lecture halls always so damn loud?

"How long have you been here?" he asks, lowering his cup.

I shrug. "Got here a couple minutes before you knocked," I lie.

Jay eyes me for what feels like forever, before a knowing smile appears on his sexy as fuck face. Seriously, why does this man have to be so damn good looking? It should be a sin to look that hot. I hate that he's able to read me so easily too. He seems to always know when I'm trying to bullshit my way out of something and he calls me on it. Every. Damn. Time.

"How long have you really been here, Katherine?"

Fuck me. the full name, really?

He had to go there. Nobody calls me Katherine, except for my mother dearest. And that's exactly why I hate it. But coming from his mouth, I think it's the sexiest damn thing I've ever heard.

A sigh escapes passed my lips when I lower my head and answer his question. "Twenty minutes."

"Now, was that so hard?" he laughs.

"Fuck you," I spit out, attempting to dramatically cross my arms until I remember the coffee cup I'm holding and refusing to give up possession of it. I'm not even sure why I said that. I think I'm just trying to be difficult and give him a tough time. Or I'm trying to cover up the way his eyes on me and that knowing smile are affecting me. It's probably the latter one.

"Baby, you know I'd be up for round two. You just gotta say the word," he teases.

"You're insatiable," I roll my eyes.

"Only when it comes to you," he concludes as we see Parker and Danielle's Subaru SUV pull up.

Bella is adorable in her tiny soccer uniform. She's still a little unsure on the field but she's a lot more confident since the time we were at the rec centre last year. Parker must have been getting her on the field a lot more this season.

Just as Bella runs by us with a wave, my phone pings with a text. I move my coffee to my other hand and dig around in my purse until my fingers wrap around the cold metal. One of these days I swear I will get a case for it, but I keep forgetting every time I'm around the mall.

Jay: You up for a trip to the range after this?
Me: Heck yes!

I'm so excited to hit the range with Jay I can't sit still anymore; my knees bounce with the thought of trying out the new gun he bought me for my birthday. It is a matte pink FMK 9C1 G2 9mm and I haven't had a chance to take it out yet in the two months I've owned it. Pink isn't normally the color I would gravitate towards but, in the case of this gun, I wouldn't trade it for the world.

It may have something to do with the person who bought it for me.

"Okay, don't laugh," I look over at Jay. "It's been a while since I've done this."

His idea of a range was to drive past the city limits to the woods in the middle of nowhere and set up some beer can targets.

"How long's a while?"

"Um, never. I've never done this," I reply, slipping my hands in the front pockets of my jeans.

Hey, I never said what kind of range I spent hours at.

He laughs like he doesn't believe me. "You've never done this?"

"I always wanted to and I do plan on getting my restricted license but I just never had the time...until now."

"Jesus, Kat. I gave you that gun thinking you already had your license. You could've told me you didn't have it yet. You know it's illegal for you to have that gun without your license?" He rakes a hand through his blond hair.

"I know, and I was going to tell you. But who better to teach me than an ex-special ops member and current RCMP officer?" I ask in the sweetest voice I can and hope that he doesn't make us leave.

He studies me for what feels like forever before he drops his hand from around the back of his neck. "Fuck. Okay, look. If anyone asks, we went to grab a couple of beers instead." He points at me. "And the gun stays at my house until you get that license."

I'm bouncing on the balls of my feet. I'm thrilled and relieved that he didn't make us leave *and* take my gun away. "Deal."

"Grab your gun then come over here."

I do what he says and take the FMK from its case before walking over to where he's standing about forty-five feet from the cans. He moves behind me placing his hands on my hips, his touch searing the skin above the waistband of my shorts.

"Stand with your legs about shoulder-width apart. Keep your knees flexed but not bent," he instructs and I do as I'm told. His hands move up my sides and lift my arms to where they're supposed to be. "Arms fully extended." After he makes sure that my hands are in the right position on the handgun, they go back to gripping my hips pressing himself into me when he whispers into my ear, "bend forward slightly at your hips."

I hear him take a sharp intake of air when I do as I'm told, his cock jumping slightly behind his zipper. Shivers rake up my body with his closeness and feeling his warm breath on my skin.

"When you're ready, take the safety off. Take a deep breath and when you exhale, pull the trigger."

I do as he says and watch as the first can falls over right after I pull the trigger.

"I did it!" I squeal as he slips the pistol from my hands and puts the safety back on.

"That was a good shot, Kat. Want to go again?" He holds the gun out to me with a raised eyebrow.

"Oh, hell yes," I grab the pistol from his hand and turn back towards the targets, getting into position and taking the safety off.

We spend the better part of the next hour shooting different targets he had brought with us. By the time we're done, my hands, shoulders and wrists are killing me, and despite the cooler temperature outside now that the sun is starting to set, I'm overheating. Every time I missed a shot or got frustrated, Jay would press himself up behind me again and correct my stance. I don't know what frustrated me more, when I missed a shot, or feeling him so close and hating myself for putting us strictly in the friends category.

He laughs when he catches me rubbing my shoulder with a pained look on my face. "A hot shower and an ice pack will work wonders on that."

"Probably," I agree. "But I was thinking more along the lines of a cold beer."

He chuckles. "Okay, get your stuff and let's go."

It doesn't take us long to gather up our belongings and locate as many of the spent shells as we could find among the fallen leaves. In no time, we're climbing into the cab of his truck.

"Thanks for letting me tag along with you," I allow my head to lazily roll against the headrest and smile over at him.

"Anytime," he smiles over at me before throwing the truck into drive and intertwining his fingers with mine on the armrest between our two seats.

This should be the time when I remove my hand and straighten up in my seat while reminding myself why this isn't a good idea. But it's been a long day and I'm exhausted. And truth be told, his touch offers a comfort that I could get used to. It makes me feel safe and wanted. It's knowing that no matter what happens I'll always have a place to come back to.

It feels like home.

That's the last thing that goes through my mind before my lids drift close, the beer forgotten.

3. DANGEROUS
Katherine

"Come in," his voice booms from behind the closed door.

My breath hitches when I push open the heavy office door. Cerulean eyes look tentatively up at me from under long dark lashes. His dark hair is neatly cropped and styled back.

"Mr. Walker."

I walk further into the large room approaching the front of his desk with my hand outstretched. "I'm Kat Young. Your new assistant."

He doesn't stand up to greet me, preferring to stay seated in the leather chair behind his desk. His nostrils flare when I slip my hand into his to shake and something close to a static shock shoots up my hand. His eyes fly to where our hands are connected before finding my face again.

Letting go of my hand he motions for me to take a seat at one of the chairs on the other side of his desk. Leaning back in his chair, he rests his elbows on the armrests and steeples his fingers in front of him, his eyes narrowing on me.

"So, Katherine, I assume the rest of my staff has been welcoming to you. I do apologize for my absence during your first week, but that trip could not have been postponed."

"It's Kat," I correct, absently playing with the bracelet around my right wrist.

"Kat," he repeats, a flicker in his blue eyes.

My name on his lips does something to my body that I can't really explain. His voice sends waves of shivers up my body. There's almost something sinister in it.

I should be paying attention to what he's saying but I'm not hearing a single word. Everything else fades away as the rest of my senses are honed in on his body. The way he carries himself, even just sitting behind his black marble desk.

The way he fills out every inch of his custom-made Italian suit. The slight stubble lining his jaw, not enough to be considered a beard but just enough to make him slightly more good looking. His lips are curled up into a smirk and it's then that I realize he's no longer speaking.

Good job, Kat. Way to make an impression with this first meeting.

"I'm sorry. What was that last part?"

"I'd like you to sit in on the meeting with the new client next week. Gail usually does it and takes the meeting minutes but she's requested that day off so you must take over for her. Will that be a problem, Kat?"

"No, Sir."

"Great. You can start gathering all the information from her after you get my coffee. A double espresso. And I need you to research the client's new hotel chain and give me everything you find."

I can feel his eyes track me as I make my way out of his office. It makes me want to cover my behind with my hands and scamper out of his office, willing him to stop looking at my ass. It's not like I'm even wearing a form fitting skirt.

During my research, I find that one of the client's new hotels houses dolphins. My heart sinks with the realization that the company I work for is supporting a business that thinks it's okay to glorify mammals in captivity. It goes against everything I stand for.

But there's a possibility that Mr. Walker might have no idea where these dolphins come from. Now I have a dilemma. Do I tell him? Do I up and quit? Or do I keep my head down and my mouth shut?

Only two of those don't go against the type of person I am, and I quite like my job. It's decided; I'll take him the information I've found and then ask if he knew where they acquire their dolphins.

My palms are sweaty as I push open his office door after I've knocked.

"I have that research you asked for," I hold up the file in front of me as I approach his desk.

"Thank you. You can just set it down." He doesn't look up from the papers he's signing.

I do as he says and place the file on his desk off to the side. I run my hands down my pencil skirt nervously and almost chicken out before straightening my spine and taking a deep breath.

"Sir? There's something in the research of their hotel chain that bothered me."

He glances up from his paperwork, his blue eyes unnerving me, his pen stopping mid-sign. "What is it?"

Suddenly, with his eyes and full attention locked on me, my throat goes dry and all thought leaves me and I can't remember what I was planning on saying. Not because I'm attracted to him, even though he's a good-looking guy, but there's something not quite right with the way he looks at me. The way his gaze rakes over my body makes me uncomfortable.

Damnit, there was a reason I brought it up...

"Kat," he prompts.

Oh right! Dolphins.

"Do you know where they get the dolphins for the aquariums at their hotels?"

He drops the pen on the stack of papers and intertwines his fingers in front of his face. "No, can't say that I do. Is there something wrong?"

This is it.

This is my opportunity to tell him about everything I've learned and researched in the last six years on this issue.

"Sir- "

"David," he corrects with a raised eyebrow.

"David," I repeat. "Any dolphins in captivity are more than ninety-percent likely to come from this cove where fishermen drive in thousands every year." I don't take a breath before continuing, in fear that he might cut me off. "Of these thousands, only a few get chosen for life in captivity in an aquarium, or swim-with-dolphin programs at a hotel or resort. The rest are brutally and inhumanely slaughtered. David, I know the financial benefits that this client could bring to your company but this is something that I've been researching and been passionate about for years. So even if you continue with this business relationship, I still had to do my part and let you know."

For the first time since I started talking I take a breath and then prepare myself for the backlash.

The backlash that never comes.

He doesn't say anything for the longest time, choosing to sit there staring at me. Finally, he drops his hands and leans back in his chair. His eyes still piercing mine.

"Well," he exhales hard, "this really is something you're passionate about, isn't it?"

"It is."

"You're right. The client could have significant financial benefits for this company."

I nod. "They could."

"Is everything in there? Including some research on that cove?" he asks, pointing one long masculine finger at the file I had placed on his desk.

"It is."

"I'll take a look at it, but I'm not promising anything," he warns.

A grin splits across my face. "Thank you."

The rest of the week goes by in a blur with phone calls, emails, scheduling and rescheduling his entire next week as things come up and others get changed.

The meeting with the new client goes off without a hitch and

I'm even surprised with myself for being able to keep up with taking notes for the minutes. It also helped that David, uh, Mr. Walker, kept repeating everyone's name when he would respond to their question or comment. I knew he was doing it for my benefit and I appreciated it. He gave me a heads up beforehand that he wasn't bringing up the dolphin issue in the meeting but promised me that he would be calling a private conference with the client to discuss it.

I'm unplugging my laptop and gathering up the charger to move back to my desk when David walks up to me and clears his throat.

"I need those minutes by the end of the day."

"That's in three hours."

He smirks, sticking one hand in his designer suit pants. "Yes. Will that be a problem, Ms. Young?"

"N-No. No problem," I stammer like a fucking idiot.

What is it with this man and my inability to form a coherent sentence. He is my boss, for god's sake! I couldn't be thinking about my boss.

Two and a half hours later, I inhale deeply through my nose before knocking on the heavy wood door to his office. My knuckles only connect with the door once before it's swinging open and then he's standing there. Looking sexy as hell.

His suit jacket isn't on and the sleeves of his white button up shirt are rolled up to his elbows, making his arms somehow look even bigger. His royal blue tie is hanging loose around his neck and the two top buttons of his shirt are undone.

"Katherine, come in." He opens the door wider before walking over to the makeshift bar on one side of the room.

"It's Kat."

"Kat," he says over his shoulder.

The hairs on the back of my neck still stand up every time I hear him say my name.

"Scotch?" he asks, holding up a crystal tumbler.

"No, I'm okay. I'm still on the job."

"Just one, and I promise I won't tell the boss," he grins.

"Just one," I laugh nervously, as he hands me a second tumbler. "Thank you, Mr. Walker."

"Please, call me David," he says, taking a seat on the couch next to the bar and gesturing for me to join him.

"David," I repeat.

He smiles approvingly and I watch as the hand holding his glass raises it up to his lips. I watch as his Adam's apple bobs with the sip.

"I have those meeting minutes you requested." I hand him the file folder.

He accepts the folder but doesn't open it, lacing it, instead, on the glass coffee table in front of us.

"You're not going to check it?"

"I trust that everything is in order. I'll read through it later if I need to."

"I'll email a copy to everyone who was present at the meeting and those who were supposed to be there but couldn't make it then," I respond, moving to get up.

"Please stay and finish your drink. The minutes can wait 'til tomorrow to be emailed," he says, placing a warm hand on my knee.

"Okay," I gulp, subtly moving my knee causing his hand to fall away.

"So, Kat. Tell me about yourself."

"Excuse me?"

"Well, I wasn't able to be at your interview and I missed your first week here at the office. You're supposed to be my assistant and I don't know you at all. So, tell me about yourself."

I watch in confusion as he gets up to refill our glasses before coming back and sitting down closer to me than he was before.

"Uh, okay. I just recently graduated with my—"

"I don't want your professional resume, Kat. I could just look that up if I needed to. I mean, tell me about you. Where did you grow up? Do you have any siblings?"

Another nervous laugh escapes before I can will it back. "Why?"

He chuckles. "Call me old fashioned but I like to get to know all my employees. That now includes you."

I give in, his reasoning makes sense. I needed to stop thinking the worst about people. "Well, I was born and raised in the GTA. Scarborough, to be exact. I'm an only child. And before you ask, no, I'm not close with my parents," I say in all one breath. I really hope that he doesn't ask why. I don't want to think of my parents right now. I put them behind me the minute I turned eighteen and moved out.

But exactly like I knew he would, he asks anyways.

"Why not?"

"Why not what?"

"Why aren't you close with your parents?"

I sigh. "Because they're not nice people and the minute I was legally old enough to, I moved out."

He doesn't say anything after that but his hand finds its way back on my knee and starts roaming up. I push his hand away and cross my legs which probably wasn't the smartest idea because his gaze heats when it lands on my bare leg.

"What about you?" I ask, hoping to distract him and draw him back into the conversation.

"What about me?" His lips pull up in a smirk.

"This whole getting-to-know-me thing is a two-way street."

His smirk morphs into a grin as he's placing his glass on the table before settling back into the couch resting his ankle over his other knee.

"All right, I was born and raised in White Rock. I have a younger brother. And my mom died from cancer several years ago."

"I'm sorry."

"Don't be. It was a long time ago."

"Is that lime I taste?" I ask after taking another sip of the smooth scotch.

He laughs, "It is. It's an twenty-year-old Glenfiddich. It has a vanilla aroma with hints of banana but then the taste has hints of lime, ginger, and spice."

"I can see why you like it."

"You do?" His hand is back to its roaming on my leg and I've about had it.

How many times do I have to keep moving his hand away before he gets the fucking message? I place my still full glass on the glass table and stand.

"I'm sorry, Mr. Walker, but it's been a long day and I need to be getting home."

"I was about to order some take-out. Why don't you stay and have a bite with me?"

Damn, this guy is persistent. I want to tell him to fuck off but he's my boss and I really like my job.

"I'm sorry, but I really have to go." I'm surprised my voice came out sounding so polite, since that's the furthest thing from I'm feeling right now.

David gets up and moves towards me, forcing me to back into the corner. His knuckles come up to graze down the side of my face. "Stay. Have dinner with me."

His lips are within inches of mine. His breath smells like scotch, and if I didn't know any better I would think that he had been drinking all day. And maybe he had.

His knuckles continue their way down the side of my neck, and then over the mound of my breast.

Fuck it. I don't need this job bad enough to sleep with my boss. Grabbing the hand roaming down one of my breasts, I twist his arm into the most uncomfortable position behind his back. Bringing my mouth close to his ear, I hiss, "don't ever touch me again."

I don't stick around long enough to hear his retort. Pushing open his office door and letting it slam closed behind me, I hightail it down the stairs to the ground floor.

4. CHILDHOOD

Katherine

My phone rings in the bottom of my purse while I'm trying to juggle an armload of grocery bags and unlock my apartment door.

"Hello?" I answer as I dump the bags on the kitchen counter.

"Kat…" As soon as I hear my father's voice I end the call and put the iPhone face down on the counter, continuing to unpack the groceries.

Serves me right for not checking the caller ID before answering.

My phone rings again but I ignore it. It's his prerogative if he wants to leave a voicemail, but nothing's changed. I'll never listen to them and I'll never call him back. The minute I walked out of my childhood house at eighteen was the minute I put him and my mother behind me. And my life is better for it.

They're my parents and I would never wish any harm to them but, as far as I'm concerned, they're not my family. I may not have been able to choose them as parents but I can choose who I call family, and my family consists of the five people who I know without a doubt would never mistreat me the way my parents had.

- Twenty-two years earlier -

This was it, I thought as I heard my mother's angry footsteps approach the closet door that I'm hiding in

"Where are you, you little brat?!" She hisses.

I squeeze my arms tighter around my legs and shut my eyes hoping, wishing I could blend in with the wood paneling at the back of the hallway closet. I pray that she won't yank open the door and find me.

I pray that my dad will come home from work and see what she is doing to me. I pray that the wood paneling will open and thrust me into a different world, *Narnia* style.

The door to the closet flies open, my mother stands on the other side and I know that this time it will be different. The purple blouse she wears make her brown eyes stand out even more and the rage I see in them makes me freeze. They are cold, uncaring of my outcome.

I caused this.

I am the cause of her rage. I ruined her life. She constantly told me that she never did want me but my dad had begged her to keep me.

"You bitch! How dare you hide from me!" She yells, grabbing my arm so tight I can feel the bruise forming instantly.

"I'm s-s-sorry momma. I d-d-didn't mean to," I whimper as she yanks me out of the closet and pushes me against the wall. I feel my neck snap forward and instantly back as I hit the cold paint and slide down.

Everything goes black and when I came to my mother is still yelling at me but I can't make out her words. I'm trying to concentrate on making the floor stop spinning but it doesn't work.

The spinning gets worse and I feel a blow to my stomach, then another. I fight to stay conscious, knowing that if I don't the kicks will just get worse and she won't stop.

"You worthless piece of shit! I didn't want you in the first place," she screams as another blow hits my ribs.

Yeah, tell me something I don't know.

I hear more than see her stomp off in the direction of the bar in the living room. The pain is so bad all I want to do is stay laying on the tile but I know that if I'm still here when she comes back there will be hell to pay.

Cringing in pain, I stand up, which is probably not the best idea since my ribs feel like they are all snapped in two but I don't want to make her angrier with me. I'll never know how I made it from that floor to my bedroom at the top of the stairs with, I would later find out, two broken ribs and a dislocated arm.

By the time I shut my door, the darkness is threatening to take over and I know that she has succeeded this time, that this was it. I would never wake up again. The prospect of finally escaping my mother's clutches makes me smile but I am angry.

I'm angry at my mother for what she did, but mostly I'm angry at my dad for not doing anything about it. I'm angry at him for letting her kill me slowly and I'm angry at him for not loving me enough to save me.

I am angry at God too. Why did he put me with these parents? A mom who can't stand the sight of me and uses me as her own personal punching bag and a dad who can't care less about what she does to me. What did I ever do to deserve this kind of punishment?

Wiping the last of the blood from my nose, I pull the blanket off my bed. Wincing from the pain, I get down on the floor and crawl under my bed, finally giving in to the pain and the dark.

My phone ringing for the fourth time in a row draws me out from the memories.

"What is it, Dad?" I ask, blowing out a breath. At least the ringing stopped.

"Kat, it's your mother."

His voice sounds different. Tired. Defeated somehow. But I don't care enough to ask how he's doing. "What is it?"

"She had a stroke, Kat. Do you…Do you think you can come home and see her?" my father's voice pleads with me.

I sigh, pinching the bridge of my nose between my thumb and forefinger. "No, Dad. I can't come home."

"Kat- "

"No. I can't. I'm sorry. Don't call again." I end the call and immediately set a do not disturb for his number.

The fact that there is even an ounce of sadness warring inside of me makes me mad. My mother was nothing special. In fact, she was a horrible mother. She made me feel like I was a burden on their lives and my father just sat back and let it happen, never once sticking up for his little girl or standing up to his wife.

It didn't take me long to realize how weak and how much of a coward my father was. The day of my eighteenth birthday I hightailed it out of there and moved. My parents never put up a fight when I told them that I was leaving, but I never expected them to. It's been ten years and I haven't heard anything from either of them - no phone calls, no emails. Until today.

Guess I should feel relieved at that. I have nothing to say to either one of them and I should be glad that they finally cannot touch me.

But I'm not relieved. I'm pissed off. How dare they think that I would just come running back the minute they called? Okay, so my mother had a stroke but my mother never gave a shit about me so why should I give a shit about her?

It might make me a bitch but I didn't care. I. Don't. Care.

But my dad didn't sound well.

Fucking Hell.

I already know that I'm going to end up going back there. Not for my mother, but for my father. He may have been a coward while I was growing up but as much as I hate it, I'll always be his little girl, and I didn't like the way his voice sounded during that phone call.

So, I'll go back but I won't be going for her. I'm only going to check on him.

After I book a ticket home for the next morning I realize that I don't want to be alone tonight so while I'm on a roll of making mistakes this week, I shoot a text off to Jason.

Me: Got a phone call from my father today.

Jay: What'd he want?

Me: He thought I should know that my mother had a stroke. He asked me to come home.

Jay: Fuck no.

That one makes me smile. He has always been my advocate. My protector. Making sure that people don't take advantage of me.

Sometimes it's stifling because I prefer to fight my own battles but other times it's nice to know that someone would go to bat for me.

Me: Can you come over? I don't really feel like being alone right now.

Jay: Be there in 30. Anything you want me to grab on the way?

Me: Alcohol.

Jay: Trying to get me into bed again, Katherine? *wink*

Me: *rolls eyes* In your dreams

Jason

"Hey," Kat says with a small smile, as she holds the door open.

I can tell she's trying to hide the fact that she has been crying. She's trying to put on a strong face so that she can convince me she really *is* fine but I know my girl and she is not fine.

"Hey" I reply, walking into her apartment.

I make a beeline for her kitchen and put the six pack in the fridge before I turn to her. "Figured we could just order from that pizza place down the street."

"Sounds good. I thought you were bringing alcohol?"

"Beer is alcohol," I smirk.

Kat rolls her eyes and I have to stifle the laugh that's bubbling up.

"When I said alcohol, I meant vodka, rum, tequila…"

"You also said that you weren't trying to get me into bed again," I waggle my eyebrows, "and we both know what happened the last time you and I partook in a little Jose."

"Ugh, touché. I'm going to hop into a quick shower. Delivery menus are in the top drawer," she calls while walking down the hall towards the master bedroom and the attached bathroom

I watch her walk away, my gaze drifting down her slender back and narrow waist, over her luscious hips and down to watch the way her ass looks in those yoga pants. I have to stifle back a groan at the memory of how it felt to have that ass in my hands.

"I ordered a Hawaiian and an all meat," I call as Kat rounds the corner into the open kitchen and living room.

Her long brown hair still wet from her shower. She's changed into skinny faded jeans and a white tank top. I can see the black lace strap from her bra peeking out beneath the straps of her tank top and it takes everything I have to not stare and swallow hard.

"Beer?" I ask while opening the fridge and reaching in to grab two of the bottles from the six pack.

"Please"

"Pizza should be here in thirty." I pop the tops off the two beers and hand one to her.

"Thanks"

I take a slug of my beer while watching her out of the corner of my eye. That shower must have helped because she seems more of herself now than when I first got here but her amber eyes still hold some sadness in them.

Kat and I have talked extensively about her past so I know that there must be a war of emotions going on inside of her. On one hand, she just found out that her mother had a stroke, but on the other hand, she never was much of a mother to Kat anyway.

Her shoulders are tense and her eyes that once held laughter are sad and brimming with unshed tears. I know that she'll never allow herself to let those tears fall. Kat will never allow herself to cry in front of anyone; she has built such a big wall around herself that she's too afraid to let anyone in and show weakness.

"Look Jay, I don't want to talk about it. So, can we please not go there?" she pleads to me, knowing where my thoughts were.

I grab my beer and head to the couch. "Then we won't talk. Pick a movie" I say, sitting down and propping my boots on the glass coffee table.

Kat sighs and plops herself down next to me snuggling in close under my arm and I fight the feeling of how right this feels and how perfectly she fits next to me.

A knock at the door saves me from continuing those thoughts. I jump up pulling out my wallet from my back pocket to pay the delivery guy before sliding the boxes onto the coffee table in front of her.

"Dig in," I motion to the pizza boxes on the table, sitting down next to her and grabbing a slice of the all meat pizza before turning back to the movie she picked out.

Beauty and the Beast plays out on her big screen TV. Kat is a Disney fanatic so it doesn't surprise me that when I told her to pick a movie she instantly went for one of her all-time favorites.

"I'm going back," she announces, still staring straight ahead at the TV.

"You're what? Why would you do that to yourself, Kat?"

Her shoulders slightly move up and down with each inhale and exhale before she looks at me. "I'm not going for her. I could care less about her. I'm going to check on my father."

"Why do you want to go at all?"

"I don't want to. I just feel like it's something I should do. Maybe I can finally get some answers from him."

"Kat," I plead as I take her hand in mine, "they might not be the answers you're looking for."

"I know," she whispers.

"How long are you going for?"

"Just a few days. I have a flight booked out for tomorrow."

"Okay." I tug her hand and pull her into me, kissing the top of her head when she leans into my chest.

Kat's phone lights up with a new message and when she leans back into the couch I catch a glimpse of the name of the sender.

"Who's David?"

"My new boss," she says almost dismissively.

"Your boss texts you at nine o'clock on a Friday night?" Now I'm intrigued. It's obvious by the way she's acting - the dismissive answers, the way she angles her phone away from me - that there's something more going on that she doesn't want to tell me.

Kat shrugs. "He's just confirming that I sent out the meeting minutes from earlier."

She places her phone face down on the arm of the couch and goes back to eating pizza and watching the movie but I can see her constantly glancing at her phone, like she's trying to stop herself from checking for a new message.

5. PROTECTOR
Katherine

On the screen, Gaston is singing about how Belle is the one he is going to marry but I'm not paying attention to any of it. I keep looking at my phone out of the corner of my eye and wondering how he got my number. Then I remember that I'm his assistant so of course he would have my cell number.

David: Go to dinner with me tomorrow night.

I didn't need to ask who it was. Only one person had asked me to go to dinner with them tomorrow night. Couldn't the guy take a hint? Was me twisting his arm not answer enough for him?

I hated myself for lying to Jay too when he glanced at the screen as I was saving David's number in my contacts. But there's no way that I could tell him about David. He would go ape shit. As much as he jokes about it, I know that secretly he wishes we were more than friends. That one night meant more to him than it did to me. I was drunk, off tequila of all things. I'm not responsible for my actions when Jose is involved.

c I like Jay. A lot. More than friends a lot. But it would never work between us. And David? David creeps me out, despite his good looks.

When he shifts on the couch I get a hint of his cologne and God, he smells so good, like spice and pure man. I inwardly cringe when my thoughts start going their normal route when it comes to him.

Friends Kat! Strictly friends!

"Another beer?" he asks, getting up and moving towards the kitchen. I raise my empty bottle in silent approval and settle my eyes back on the screen, determined in my resolve to be his friend.

Ten minutes later, the door to my apartment flies open and Alice waltzes through. She drops her purse on the hallway table and her keys in the glass bowl in the center of it, then plops herself down next to me and grabs a slice of pizza before leaning back.

"Thought you were closing," I comment.

"Closed early. It was dead and I was bored so Jer said to just close it down.”

I shoot my gaze over to Jay before settling back into the couch and returning my attention to the Disney movie playing out on my TV. That doesn't last long, though, because I hear an exasperated sigh coming from next to me and I automatically start preparing for what I know is coming next.

“Let's go out tonight!” Alice exclaims.

Yup, called it.

“I need a night out with my best friends. I just wrote the hardest exam of my life today and had one of the most boring shifts at the café. I could do with a fun Friday night out,” she says, looking from me to Jay and back again.

“I don't know.”

“Come on Kat. Please!”

“I'm in.” He smiles

Shit! Really?

If they're all going, then I'll have to go. Alice won't let me stay home by myself on a Friday night.

Damnit!

“Don't be a party pooper, Kat,” Alice says, her eyes pleading with me to do this for her.

I sigh knowing that I'm going to give into her eventually. Nobody has ever said no to Alice and how could they when she looks at them with those honey-brown puppy dog eyes.

“Where's Mike?” she asks, noticing for the first time that he isn't here.

“Apparently, he had a date tonight” I state.

Alice's eyes go wide and I see a pang of hurt flash across them before she covers as if it never happened.

What the fuck was that? Mike and Alice? And why would she not tell me.

I'll have to ask Jay about Alice and Mike later when we're by ourselves.

“He's not with the blonde Barbie, is he?” she asks, turning to

Jay. Jay, Parker, and Mike were childhood friends then joined the RCMP together.

I shoot Jay a questioning look while Alice has her head turned. He just shrugs it off. Her gaze swings over to me again and I see that same pleading look in her eyes for me to go out with them tonight.

"Fine," I concede.

She bounces up and down with a huge smile across her face. "We can check out that new club that just opened up. I've heard that it's supposed to be the hot new thing. We'll cab it!" she says, jumping up and heading in the direction of my shower. I swear the girl just makes herself at home anywhere.

I slump back into the back of the couch. This should be an interesting night. I hate going to the club. All those sweaty bodies in a cramped space, drunk people bumping into you, and pervs trying to rub up onto you. It wouldn't be bad if it was just dancing.

It's also how he and I ended up naked in bed together.

I shiver just thinking about it but Alice needs me so I'll go for her and plus I could use a drink…or two. I glance at my phone and notice that it's already ten.

"Go get ready. I'm going to run home and shower and be back here in an hour to pick you girls up." He stands, moving towards the door and with a final wave he's gone.

Jason

After I let my eyes adjust to the low light of the club, I feel like I just walked into a circus. In the four corners of the club there are long white sheets hanging from the ceiling to the floor with a blue light cast on each, turning the sheet from white to purple. Rolling down from the top are women dressed in very colorful leotards with no safety lines.

In the center is a makeshift stage with more women in skin tight leotards acting out a scene with some of those ribbon-on-a-stickthingies. Closer to the ceiling are gymnastic swings.

The bartender is wearing black slacks, no shirt, and a black blazer with black eye makeup. The servers are all women decked out in black short shorts, white tank tops, and sleeveless coat tail jackets. All of them have glittery eye makeup and little top hats resting on their heads with the string going under their chins. I smirk to myself.

Well, okay then, drinks and a show it is.

"So, this place is...different," Kat says as we're lead to our corner booth where Mike is already waiting.

"I told you they change the theme every couple months. I guess this time it's a twist on the usual circus" Alice shrugs.

"I'm not complaining," Mike says as his gaze rakes over a couple of the female servers walking by our booth.

"Me neither," I chime in, sliding into the booth opposite Mike.

"As long as no clowns jump out at me," Kat adds.

When one of the servers comes to take down our drink order, she doesn't hesitate to order her favorite drink, a Blue Hawaiian.

Well, it's not tequila.

After a couple drinks, Alice jumps up and drags Kat out of her seat with a high pitched, "let's dance!"

Kat groans as Alice leads her to the outer edge of the dance floor and turns around so that her back is facing our table. The alcohol must have hit her system between the time Alice dragged her out of our booth and the time they hit the dance floor because when Alice starts dancing Kat joins her and by the second song she looks like she's having fun.

I take another long pull of my beer and try to ignore the fact that Kat looks damn good on that dance floor in that skin-tight red dress and ignore the fact the I want to kick the ass of every guy in this club with their eyes glued to her.

It takes everything I have to unclench my fist and will myself to not go over there and wrap my arms around her and claim her as mine. I look over at Mike and it looks like he's thinking along the same lines.

We've both been protective over those girls, but somewhere along the line it became about more than that for me with Kat.

"How'd the date with Erin go?" I ask him trying to focus my mind on something other than Kat in that dress and the guy that just danced up to them.

"Shit," Mike stammers under his breath shaking his head and slamming back the rest of his beer.

"That good, huh?" I grin

"She wants me to meet her parents this week," he says shaking his head. "I don't do parents."

I laugh. "Dude, you don't do relationships, period."

He holds up a new glass of beer. "Cheers to that" he grunts, and slams it back.

I shake my head; in all the years I've known Mike, he has never once had a committed relationship. He doesn't do relationships; he only does one-nighters. He's part of the "love 'em and leave 'em" club and he doesn't seem to be eager to change that anytime soon.

He slams his glass down on the table and tilts his head towards the dance floor where two more guys have come up to Alice and Kat and have pulled the girls in too close for my comfort.

"Enough of this," Mike barks and slides out of the booth heading in their direction, and I'm hot on his heels.

Katherine

I feel two beefy arms grip my hips and the heavy stench of tobacco and alcohol coming off the guy in front of me makes me want to hurl.

"Hey darlin'," he rasps.

I open my eyes and look up into his round face. His eyes are cold and a devilish smile tugs the corners of his lips. I struggle to get out of his grip but he holds me tight bringing me closer to him.

"Aw, c'mon. Dance with me" he drawls.

"Let me go." I start struggling harder as he starts moving us further to the opposite side of the dance floor. He doesn't get far before I hear a deep male voice behind me.

"Lady said to let her go"

I tilt my head to the side and see Jay stalking towards us like a man on a mission, anger clear in his emerald eyes. I turn back to the man who still has his hands firmly on me but he's gone statue-like, eyes wide and fear evident across his face. His arm instantly drops from mine.

"Sorry, dude. Should keep your lady in line better," he mutters before walking away into the crowd.

What the…He did not just say that!

Before my mouth has time to catch up with my brain, the guy is laid out on the floor and Jay's anger is palpable as he stands over him, chest heaving.

Oh fuck!

I look around. Everyone has stopped dancing and there's a crowd gathering to watch us. Putting my hand on his arm I try to reassure him that I'm okay but he doesn't feel it.

"Say that again, you piece of shit!" Jay taunts. My gaze quickly scans the crowd for backup but Alice and Mike have disappeared.

Where the hell are they?

I really hope that this idiot isn't dumb enough to answer him. I let out the breath I didn't know I was holding when the guy wisely gets up and retreats without saying another word.

"Jay, I'm really okay. Can we just go b— "

Before I can finish my sentence, he spins me around and wraps his large hand around my arm dragging me further on to the dance floor with him. When we reach the center, he spins towards me and plants both hands on my hips bringing me closer so our bodies are pressed together. I can feel his warm breath on my ear and the scent of his cologne, Dior Homme, wraps around me.

"Are you okay?" he whispers in my ear.

I nod but bury my head into his neck, not wanting to see the disappointed look in his eyes. How could I be so stupid to think that I could go out wearing this dress and just have fun?

I'm such an idiot.

As if sensing my warring thoughts, his finger lifts my chin so that I'm forced to look up at him. "You didn't do anything so stop thinking whatever it is you're thinking."

I look him hard in the eyes and the disappointed look I thought I would see there is nowhere to be found. In fact, the only thing I see is concern staring back at me.

Leaning my head back down, I snake my arms around his neck and breathe him in. He smells so good. He moves his hands from around my hips and curls his arms around my waist bringing me closer. I can feel him hard against my stomach.

I gasp and look up at him, heat and longing clear in his eyes. Before I can say anything his mouth crashes down on mine, hot and seeking, I melt into him, opening for him and his tongue clashes with mine. His teeth nip at my bottom lip and I whimper. Before I can explore the kiss any more, he pulls back.

"Christ...Kat" he says, running his hand through his blond hair causing some to spill out over his forehead. "I'm sorry, I don't know why that happened." He refuses to look at me, instead shaking his head and avoiding eye contact. "I'll get Mike to take you girls home," he says before stalking off leaving me standing there in shock, head spinning from that kiss.

What the hell just happened?

I make my way back to the table, where I find Mike and Alice. Before I even sit down across from Alice, I drain the remain liquid from my glass.

"What the hell happened? Jay practically ran out of here," she asks

"Some jerk started getting cocky. Jay got pissed, told the guy to leave me alone," I shrug, surprised that I managed to keep my voice sounding normal before starting in on the new cocktail the server just set down in front of me.

When I look up again, I can see on her face that Alice knows that isn't the whole story but she chooses not to pursue it here in front of Mike. Instead, she reaches over to grab his beer and takes a long sip before putting it back down in front of him, giving me a shy smile. He just narrows his eyes at her not saying anything.

"I'm going to get going. I have an early flight out tomorrow."

"Still need me to drive you to the airport in the morning?" Alice asks, stealing his beer again.

"Seriously, woman, get your own damn beer," he huffs, but Alice just sticks her tongue out at him then smiles.

He tries to hide the smile that's threatening to pull at his mouth but he's not doing a very good job.

"Sure, if you still can that would be great."

"I'll be there with coffee."

"And that's why we're best friends," I say, grabbing my clutch.

When I'm heading out to the waiting cab my phone pings.

David: Heard you requested a few days off.

Me: I did. Family emergency back home.

David: What time's your flight?

Me: 7 am

David: Let me take you to the airport

Me: I already have a ride

David: Cancel it

Resting my head against the back seat of the cab, I turn the ringer off on my phone, not replying to his text. This has all just gotten too confusing and the rum isn't helping. I didn't report David to HR, even though I know I should have. I figured that I could deal with it. I would handle it on my own and it would go away. But the man is persistent, and keeps texting me.

As soon as I throw my clutch down on the couch and kick off my heels there's a knock on my door.

Who the hell would be coming over at almost two in the morning.

Standing on my tippy toes I look out of the peep hole. David is standing on the other side of my door, one hand leaning on the door frame the other hand in his dark jeans.

"What are you doing here?" I ask pulling open the door.

"Cancel your ride," he says pushing past me and walking into the apartment.

"Please, come in," I sigh, closing the door behind him. "I'm not cancelling my ride and you can't be here."

"Nice apartment." He ignores what I said, slowly walking around the open living room, randomly picking up picture frames to get a closer look then putting them back.

"What are you doing here, David?"

"I already told you." He puts down the final picture frame he was examining then turns to face me.

It's a little unnerving having all six-feet-two inches of him focused on me. Despite the jeans and polo shirt he's wearing he still looks perfectly put together. His jet-black hair is perfectly styled, even at two in the morning.

Does this man ever sleep?

His cerulean-blue eyes darken as they rake over my body before finding my face again. "You went out in that?"

My arms unwillingly cross over my body. I feel too exposed in this dress, especially in front of David. I shift my weight from foot to foot uncomfortably when he stalks closer to me.

I don't want his eyes on me, nor his hands either so I take a step back when he moves closer.

"Don't," he commands as he reaches out and slowly untangles my arms from my body. "Don't hide your body from me."

"Why are you here, David?"

The hairs on the back of my neck stand up when he tightens his grip on my wrists.

"You look beautiful." His tongue comes out to lick his lips as his eyes slowly roam over my breasts.

"You're hurting me." I try to twist my wrists and pull them back towards my body but his grip tightens.

He has us backed against the wall separating my living room from my bedroom. His one hand travels up my arm and cups my neck while his thumb slides across my bottom lip.

"Cancel your ride," he says again.

"No." Even I can hear how scared my voice sounds.

He leans in and licks a spot behind my ear. "Cancel your ride, Katherine."

My breathing picks up when my back is forced against the wall and he presses himself more into me, his grip still solid around my wrist. David grips my chin with his other hand and forces his mouth down on mine, demanding entry. Tears roll down my face while I try to rip my face out of his hands with no avail.

His hand finally leaves my chin to make its way down my stomach and around my back to cup my ass. I finally break away from his kiss and use my one hand to pound on his chest.

"David, stop. Please," I beg, but his hand continues its assault on my ass and his mouth trails down my neck. My fist is still pounding on his chest when my front door flies open.

"What the fuck!"

In the next second, David is being yanked off me and Jay stands in between us, his shoulders heaving. If he were a cartoon character, I'm pretty sure there'd be steaming coming out of his ears. My fingers tremble when I try to hold the broken strap of my dress together to keep from falling down and exposing one of my breasts.

"Who are you?" David sneers, wiping the blood from his nose with the back of his hand.

"The guy who's about to kick your ass," Jay snarls.

"Yeah? I'd like to see you try."

"Sure, if you have a death wish," Mike's voice carries from my front door, a dark look crossing his face.

"Get him out of here," Jay demands and Mike nods.

David tries to fight Mike but another hit to the face has him knocked out and Mike throws his limp body over his shoulder. I'm too busy watching Mike heft David out of my apartment that I don't realize Jay is studying me until his fingers graze my skin and I jump.

"Whoa, it's just me." He immediately removes his hand at my reaction. "Are you okay?"

I nod but don't chance speaking because I know that if I were to open my mouth right now I may just break down. Instead I slip my arms around Jay's waist and bury my face in his chest. I spend the next few minutes just allowing his scent to envelope me. I allow it to comfort me.

"What are you doing here? I mean, not that I'm not grateful that you happened to show up at the right time but after the way you left the club. . . ." I ask with my face still partially buried in his chest.

"Mike called and said he had noticed an odd car following your cab out of the parking lot. He thought it might've been me since mine's in the shop and I had to rent one. I was already on my way over here when he called." Jay places his hand on my arms and leans away slightly to get a better look at my face. "I didn't like the way I left."

"I'm glad you showed up when you did." I smile tentatively up at him.

I love Jason. He's my best friend. I know that if I ever needed anything, regardless of the time of day, he would do everything in his power to help me. He would protect me with his life. He takes care of me, and I him. But I can't be in love with him. It would just never work out between us.

"Who was that anyway?"

"Nobody important," I try to brush it off.

"Kat, the guy had you pinned against the wall for Christ's sake."

"I know, and you stopped it before it could go further. Thank you for that."

We stand there staring at each other; me trying to will him to drop it, and him trying to will me to explain further. Finally, Jay backs down and glances at the black watch on his wrist. "It's three in the morning. If you're sure you're okay, then I'm going to go."

"Oh. It is?" *Where the hell did the last hour go?* "Um, well can you…I mean will you…" I sigh and try again, "do you mind sleeping on my couch tonight. Please?"

He looks pointedly at me. "Okay, but I'm not sleeping on your couch."

"What? Why? Please don't leave me alone tonight."

The corner of his mouth lifts in a half smile as his eyes dart to my bedroom door and back to me.

"Jay –" I sigh.

He holds up his hands in a gesture of surrender. "We'll just sleep."

I cross my arms, lean on my left foot, and raise an eyebrow at him.

He laughs. "Katherine, I'm not fitting my six-foot-six ass on that tiny couch of yours." He drops his arms and takes a couple steps back. "I promise I'll try my best not to maul you in my sleep," he teases.

"Fine," I huff, spinning on my heels and leading the way into my bedroom.

I change into my short sleep shorts and tank top before climbing into bed but he climbs in fully clothed. A part of me is relieved because if he had stripped down to his boxer-briefs, I wouldn't have been able to control myself anymore.

As soon as I lay down and pull the duvet over myself he wraps his arm around me and I snuggle my back into his front. Sleep claims me instantly and five o'clock comes way too fast.

I'm not ready to give up the warmth of being wrapped up in his arms yet, but if I'm going to get to the airport in time for the six a.m. check-in time then I only have half an hour before I have to leave.

"Good morning," he says, his lips close to my ear.

"I don't wanna get up," I groan.

He chuckles, "You have to or you're going to miss your flight."

"That sounds like a great idea. If I miss my flight, then I'll have an excuse not to go home."

He laughs, throwing the covers off us and I almost smack him when the cool air hits my bare skin. "Come on. If you get up now, I'll grab us coffee."

"Fine, I'm up. You said the magic word: coffee."

Before I forget, I send Alice a quick message telling her not to worry about driving me to the airport.

Alice: Girl, I love you even more now for not dragging my lazy ass out of bed at the ass crack of dawn.

Alice: Be strong! Don't let them get to you. I'll have a shot of Jose waiting for you when you land in a few days. Luv u!

Me: LYH

6. VISIT TO THE PAST
Katherine

Nausea sits like a ball in my stomach as I get off the elevator on the hospital floor where my mom's room is located. Almost immediately I spot my dad. He looks older, not the kind of older that comes naturally as one ages but the kind that comes from years of stress.

He looks fragile, and not at all like the man I remember my father being. His outer appearance matches that of what I believed his inner appearance was all those years ago. Weak.

When he turns away from the nurses station his eyes collide with mine. Confusion, realization, happiness, and then sadness all flash across his eyes, one right after the other. Finally, regret settles in them as he walks towards me.

"Kat."

"Hi, Dad."

He moves to hug me but half way he must realize that I wouldn't have been receptive to it because he immediately pulls back.

"I thought you weren't coming."

"So did I."

We both stand in the hallway awkwardly looking at each other. My dad's face is a contradiction of emotions; a small smile pulls at his mouth but sadness and regret are still evident in his eyes. Eyes that look exactly like mine.

"So, is Mom's room down here?" I ask, pointing to the hallway on the right.

He confirms that it is and leads us down the hall. When he comes to a door with the number 406 he stops with his hand on the door knob.

"Kat, I - "

"Dad, please don't," I shake my head interrupting him. I don't want to hear what he's got to say right now.

I just barely psyched myself up enough to walk into the hospital and get on the elevator. I'm still nauseated just thinking about seeing my mother for the first time in ten years. I'm not ready to hear my dad's explanation or whatever he has to say right now. Maybe tomorrow I'll be more willing to hear him out but not today.

He drops his head reluctantly before turning the knob and pushing open the door.

The woman sitting up in the hospital bed still looks exactly like my mother. This woman just had a stroke and has been in the hospital for several days, yet she made sure that her dark hair is perfectly styled, not a hair out of place and no grey either, and her makeup is expertly done. She's not even wearing the usual hospital gown they give every patient. No, not my mother. She's wearing her own silk pajamas from home.

Her brown eyes widen in shock when I step through the door in front of my father. "Katherine. Well, what a surprise."

"Hello, Mother."

"What brings you back to the GTA after all these years?"

I'm not even sure if she wants me to answer her because she went right back to examining her nail beds after that initial greeting.

"I heard you were sick. I came to see how you were doing."

Her head snaps up so fast I fear that she may have given herself whiplash.

"I'm not sick, Katherine. I had a stroke. And since when do you care how I or your father are doing. We haven't heard a word from you since you left all those years ago."

I can feel heat start to crawl up my back and my spine stiffen. "Well, do you blame me?"

"What ever are you talking about? We're your parents, Katherine. And it seems you couldn't have been bothered to take five minutes out of your day to call us and let us know you're okay."

"Excuse me? What ever am I talking about? You're kidding, right? You know exactly what I'm talking about, Mother. Don't try and act like the concerned parent now."

"Oh, are you still on that? You were a child for god's sake. If I didn't discipline you, who knows how you would've turned out." She waves her perfectly manicured hand dismissively at the subject.

"Discipline? You call beating me within an inch of my life - twice - discipline?"

"Kat, please. Keep your voice down," my dad pleads from his seat on the other side of my mother's bed.

"No, Dad. I won't keep my voice down. It's about time someone stood up to her and since you were never going to do it."

"Katherine, please. Stop being so dramatic," my mother says, rolling her eyes.

I honestly don't know why I even bothered to come back. I knew that after ten years nothing would have changed. It was just a waste of time and money. I feel like an idiot for even thinking that I could come back and get the answers I was looking for all these years. I feel like an idiot for thinking that maybe she would be remorseful about what she had done and the way she treated me. But most of all, I feel like an idiot for thinking that my dad might apologize for not standing up for me and protecting me all those years ago. Jay was right; I shouldn't have come.

Without saying another word to either of them, I straighten up to my full height, pull the strap of my purse higher on my shoulder and walk out of the hospital room with my head held high.

As I'm getting into a cab, my phone lights up with Jay's name on the caller ID.

"Hey."

"How'd it go, Kat?"

"Well, I've been here all of five hours and I'm ready to come home," I sigh into my phone watching as the city buildings morph into highway outside the window.

"When's your scheduled flight out?"

"Day after tomorrow. Jay, you were right. This whole trip was a waste of time. I was never going to get the answers I was looking for. Hell, I was barely in the same room as them for more than ten minutes."

"Are you staying in Toronto?"

"It's not like I have a choice. I can't afford to change my ticket. It's fine though. Just because I'm stuck here doesn't mean I have to see them again. I could go exploring. You know, do the whole be-a-tourist-in-your-town thing."

He laughs. "You could. You always wanted to go up the CN Tower but were never able to."

"This is very true, sir. And I could spend a day at Casa Loma."

"Sounds like fun."

"Oh, tons," I grin.

He and I talk until the cab drops me off at my hotel and I'm in the elevator heading up to my room. When I get off on my floor there's someone leaning against the door to my room. As I get closer, realization dawns. I would recognize this man anywhere.

"Jay?"

He straightens up, slipping his phone back in the inside pocket of his suit jacket.

"What are you doing here?" I ask confused. I had just gotten off the phone with him and he never mentioned being here. Also, I don't think I've ever seen him in a suit other than at Danielle and Parker's wedding. But he looks sexy as hell. My mouth waters at the way he fills out the suit.

"I had a last-minute business meeting in Toronto. I thought I would take you to dinner."

Oookay, Jay was RCMP so I wasn't sure what he meant by business meeting, *but I figure that if he wants me to know he'll tell me so I shrug it off.*

"How'd you know I'd be staying here?" I ask, sliding the key card into the reader and pushing open the door.

He doesn't say anything just smirks and raises an eyebrow.

"Dani," I guess.

He chuckles. "There's very little that woman doesn't know."

"It almost scares me how much information she can get in a

short amount of time. Water?" I ask, opening the small bar fridge and offering him one of the bottled waters. He takes it and sits down on the end of the king size bed.

"So, dinner?"

I groan. I want to do dinner with him, I do. But that meeting with my parents took a lot out of me and I was honestly just looking forward to getting back into my pajamas, ordering room service, and gorging myself on chocolate and ice cream, only to slip under the covers afterward and not emerge until late the next morning.

But if Jay was offering, then who am I to deny him?

I kick off my heels and sit in the office chair pulling my knees up in front of me. "Fine, you can buy me dinner on two conditions."

"Okay, shoot."

I hold up a finger, "one, we order dinner and eat in here. And two," I hold up a second finger, "you order a couple bottles of wine to go with it."

He raises a questioning eyebrow and I'm sure he's not going to agree to my first condition. I'm not even sure of the last time he just ate dinner in front of the TV, but he surprises me.

"Deal."

"You serious?"

"I have one condition though."

"What's that?"

"You let me do the ordering."

"I can live with that. I should warn you, though. I'm a picky eater."

He tips his head back and laughs. "Fairly sure I'm already aware of that."

"Great, I'm going to go shower."

When I walk out of the bathroom I'm stunned speechless. Various takeout containers litter the desk, both night stands, and a pizza box sits on the bed. It's like a *Gilmore Girls* dinner.

"What's all this?"

"There's Chinese, pizza, sushi, Thai, and Indian," he smiles, looking impressed with himself.

"Did you buy out a buffet?" I tease, looking around at all the food.

"Oh, and the most important part. A white zinfandel and a moscato," he says, pulling two wine bottles from behind his back.

"I think I love you!" I grab the Moscato from his hand and waste no time in prying the cap open and filling one of the wine glasses to the brim.

"Long day?" he inquires, watching me.

"You have no idea," I respond after taking a healthy sip. God, that tastes so good. And he managed to get my favorite brand. too. This was why we're best friends.

"So where are you starting with food?"

I glance at my glass of wine and then to all the take-out containers. While I normally love spicy food, tonight is not one of those nights so I automatically veto the Thai and Indian food. "I'll start with sushi. The pizza will come in handy to soak up all this alcohol later."

"Sushi, it is then." He moves the pizza box to the table and grabs the sushi containers before sitting on one side of the bed scooting up to lean against the headboard. He inclines his head to the side in a silent invitation for me to join him. And after grabbing the TV remote, I do.

"Do you mind if we watch the hockey game?" I ask settling in against the stack of pillows.

He shakes his head. "No, I almost forgot there was a game tonight. Who's playing?"

"Vancouver and Edmonton."

We sit in silence for the next three periods just eating the sushi he ordered for us and watching the game. The Vancouver Canucks win with a 3-2 lead over the Edmonton Oilers.

I'm not usually much of a hockey fan - *I know shocker for a Canadian to not be a hockey fan* - but I needed those two and a half hours to get back to a somewhat normal version of myself after that interaction with my parents earlier today. The next best thing to getting into a ring and punching out my anger and frustration is to watch hockey, and it isn't a hockey game without a couple fights thrown in for good measure.

"I don't remember the last time I did this," he casually announces next to me while he turns the TV off.

"What's that?"

"Had a dinner that wasn't at my desk, at a pub, or at Parker's with the whole gang."

"You've never just eaten dinner lounging in front of the TV?" I can't imagine that anybody doesn't do that at least once a week. Hell, it's a regular occurrence at my place.

"I never said never," he smirks and shrugs one shoulder, "but it's been years. I probably haven't since before I joined the military."

"I find it a little hard to believe that you never eat dinner at home."

"I never realized it before now but yeah, it's been a while since I've spent any time at home other than to sleep, shower, and change."

His eyes find mine and his mouth quirks up in a small smile.

"And you're not tired of it? The long days and nights?"

"It's what I always wanted to do, even as a kid. And there was never really anyone to come home to."

"Never a girlfriend?"

He smirks shaking his head. "There was one. We were together for a couple years but she couldn't handle my constant absence. I didn't exactly beg her to stay either."

"I don't know how you do it."

I couldn't imagine the kinds of things the teams see every day, let alone the types of things Jay saw when he was on deployment.

"When it's something you love, something you're passionate about, you'll do *anything* to see it succeed and when it does there's no other feeling like it."

"Do you regret it?" my voice is barely above a whisper.

"Do I regret what?"

"The long hours. Not having a family or even a girlfriend."

"No."

We spend hours just sitting on the king size bed in my hotel room talking. He tells me a bit more about his time in the military, and his special ops unit. He tells me about his parents and how close they were as a family, and how a car accident left him and Steven orphans. A distant aunt and uncle ended up adopting them both, but they were forever changed after their parents were taken away so suddenly.

He threw himself into his school work and was determined to make his aunt and uncle happy by getting high grades. His brother Steven rebelled, getting into drugs and drinking at the age of fifteen. Thankfully, after he graduated high school, Steven cleaned up and is doing well for himself now.

I tell him a little more about my childhood. There isn't a whole lot left to tell since Jay arguably knows me better than anyone else. I hate the way people's behavior changed towards me when they found out my mother used to hit me. I hate their sympathetic looks and how they think I can't hear them when I turn away and have my back facing them.

I'm not some fragile thing. Yes, my mother was abusive and for a while I was depressed and angry. You could even say I was a little revengeful. I wanted her to get whatever she had coming to her. In the end, I made myself sick over it. Still, I couldn't change my past. I couldn't change what happened to me and what I had to endure for my entire childhood until I was sixteen and she realized she couldn't beat me anymore.

But I could change my future.

That's where my crazy need for control came into play. I couldn't control my past but I could control my future. Or I could try. I know that some things are just going to be out of my control. I couldn't, and didn't want to, control what others did or didn't do. But my actions, my thoughts, my circumstances, those were all things I could.

That was a joke. I needed to be in control of those things yet I wasn't because of a little thing called anxiety. It was a bitch.

Some days were okay and others weren't. Most days it took everything in me to just get out of bed or to leave my house. To the rest of the world I looked and acted normal. I never let on to anybody that I struggled to leave my apartment on a daily basis. Or that going out and being social took a huge toll on me, emotionally. People thought that the only reason why I couldn't come out one day was because I had a lot of work to do. But that wasn't it at all. I needed that day to myself. I needed that day to be alone, to give my anxiety a reprieve.

It sucked and I hated it.

When the alarm on my phone goes off, he and I are shocked to learn that we stayed up until seven just talking. I'm even more surprised to see that the wine bottle I had opened only had two glasses poured from it and I hadn't even touched my wine glass since the hockey game ended the night before.

The minute realization dawns as to why that alarm was set, I quickly turn it off and shove it back into the front pocket of my jeans. I try to hide my pain and disappoint but he catches it.

"What did you have planned today?"

"I was supposed to go back to the hospital and spend some time with my parents," I sigh, "but that's not happening. I think I may go do some exploring though."

"Need a guide?"

"Don't you have a team to get to?"

He shakes his head as he gets up from the bed. "I had planned on heading back to BC this afternoon but I think I can postpone it."

"No," I protest, swinging my legs over the edge of the bed, "don't stay because of me. If you need to get back, you should go."

He walks around the bed to me and cups my face between his palms, "There's nothing scheduled that couldn't wait a couple days. Get some sleep. I'll be back to pick you up around noon," he places a soft kiss on my forehead before moving to the door.

Jay picks me up from my hotel room at noon, as promised. We walk down the street to a small Italian bakery to grab a quick lunch before starting our exploration of the city.

I love the big city. I love how insignificant it makes me feel with its tall buildings and fast-paced lifestyle. I don't miss living in it but I miss the feel of it.

He starts us off with two tickets to the double-decker, hop-on hop-off red bus tour. We take it to the Hockey Hall of Fame and get a picture with the Stanley Cup before hopping back on and taking it to the Bata Shoe Museum.

Yes, I did drag this man into a museum filled with shoes and I didn't feel guilty about it. He got hockey, I got shoes. It seemed like a fair trade.

We spend hours exploring Casa Loma and its grounds. This was probably my favorite thing about Toronto. During my mom's endless beatings and degrading remarks, I would picture myself living here before it became a museum. I would picture what it would've felt like to run around the grounds outside without a care in the world. I would imagine the dances they would have in the ballroom and picture all the women in their fancy dresses. It was the only thing that got me through those dark years.

Jay and I take a ton of pictures along the way and then head to the CN Tower as our final stop before taking a dinner break. Since it's still early September and most of the summer tourists have already left, the line isn't as ridiculous as it would normally be. But we still wait in the line for an hour before we're able to take the elevator up.

My jaw drops when we walk up to the window and see downtown Toronto spread out under us. The city looks gorgeous from up here. I can't believe I used to live here and had never made it up the tower until now.

I feel Jay walk up behind me and slip his arms around my waist as I look out over the city.

"We could eat dinner at the restaurant up here."

At the mention of The 360 Restaurant my stomach does a summersault and I get queasy. Suddenly, looking down more than a thousand feet isn't so appealing anymore. I have to take a couple steps back forcing him to do the same. The restaurant got its name because it revolves 360 degrees. It's just not something I could see myself enjoying.

"Nah, I'm good. We can head down now if you're done."

I'm trying to act normal, like the thought of rotating three-hundred-sixty degrees more than a thousand feet in the air doesn't scare the crap out of me. But Jay isn't buying it. In fact, a knowing grin appears on his face.

"Or we could check out the EdgeWalk," he teases.

My arms fold across my chest and I give him my best not-impressed look but it makes him laugh harder. The bastard.

"All right, don't scowl so hard. Your face might get stuck like that."

"Ha ha, very funny. Guess you missed the day when they were handing out a sense of humor," I throw back at him while we try to make our way through the small crowd that has gathered and back to the elevator.

"I guess so," he responds placing a hand on my lower back and guiding me through.

I love the way his hand feels there; it's subtly possessive but comforting all the same.

By the time we make it down to the main floor and back out to the street, the last double-decker red bus is just pulling up to the stop so we hop on and make our way up to the open second floor.

He photobombs the selfie I'm trying to take then grabs my phone and slips it into the front pocket of his jeans, refusing to give it back to me when I ask for it. Instead, he cups my face in his palm and leans in to kiss me. I instantly melt into him. Just like that, we slip into our own little world as the bus drives through the downtown core.

When we get in the elevator of the hotel, we're a tangle of limbs as our lips lock together. He backs me into the back wall and raises both my hands above my head, holding them there with one of his and pinning me in with his hips. The kiss is possessive and full of promise.

I wrap my legs around his waist as he carries me out of the elevator when it stops on my floor. The lock on my door disengages when the key card in the back pocket of my jeans bumps against the handle.

He lifts his head and grins. "Did you just open the door with your ass?"

"Sure did," I laugh, kicking the door closed with my foot before my back is pressed against the wall and he continues his exploration of my body, slipping his hand up and under my tank top.

Right about now would normally be the time where my mind starts racing and I start talking myself out of going further with Jay but it's silent. There are no racing thoughts, no self guilt trips.

Jay's tongue suddenly flicking across my nipple pulls a moan from my throat, causing the fingers I had sliding through his hair to fist, pulling his mouth closer to my body.

"Easy, tiger," he chuckles, grabbing both of my hands and pinning them to the wall with one of his, while the fingers of his other hand trails up my jean clad thigh, and around to grip my ass as his hard cock presses harder against me, eliciting another moan from my lips.

He releases my hands, moving us away from the wall and dropping us on to the neatly-made bed. Jay slides my tank top up until it's just barely above my breasts before his mouth is back on my skin trailing sweet kisses down the middle of my chest, stomach, on either side of my belly button. His fingers expertly undo the button of my pants before his mouth is back there, following his hands as he slowly thumbs my jeans down my legs and off.

My breath hitches when he places a soft kiss on my clit over my panties before slowly removing those too. A groan escapes when his tongue runs over the sensitive bud.

"Ah, fuck!" My fingers grip the sheet on either side of me as my back arches slightly when he slides two fingers into my wet pussy.

Jay's mouth finds mine in a heated kiss, only breaking away when he lifts me up slightly to pull off my shirt and bra, and his shirt follows. I can't get enough of his kisses as my fingers fumble with his belt buckle and then his zipper.

"I need you inside of me, Jay," I pant as I push his jeans off past his round ass.

As soon as his jeans are off, he's on me again and entering me. My legs wrap around his waist, and I use my feet on his ass urging him to go harder, faster. Jay groans and fucks me harder when my nails dig into his shoulders, his teeth pulling at my nipples before his tongue licks away the sting.

The only thing going through my mind right now is how much I love having this man's hands and mouth worshiping every inch of my body.

When he looks at me it's like he only sees me. We walked around a crowded downtown Toronto today and I never once caught him checking out another woman. When we were together, I didn't feel like a second choice, or like he was only spending his day with me because he had nothing else to do. It was the complete opposite; he cancelled things so that he could spend his day with me. This man who, to my knowledge, hasn't taken a day off in almost ten years took one off so that I wouldn't have to do the tourist thing by myself.

I think I'm becoming addicted to the way his eyes light up when he sees me, and his easy laugh when we're spending time together. Or the way he gets my sarcasm and gives it back to me in spades. He subtly takes control but not in a way that makes my anxiety ramp up, or makes me want to flee for safety.

I have never stayed up all night talking to someone who wasn't one of my best girlfriends. It was different. Refreshing. And when he wrapped his arm around my shoulders while we were on the tour bus I felt safe. Like nothing could ever touch me when he was near.

My body detonates when Jay hits that spot a few more times, then I'm free falling from the best high there ever is while still sober.

"Holy shit," Jay mutters as the walls of my pussy convulse around him, and he comes.

7. JUST A FOOL
Katherine

Jason: Dinner tonight? My treat.

Me: Dinner sounds perfect. Have you checked your pants pocket yet?

He doesn't respond right away so I'm assuming he's rummaging through all of his pockets.

A smile splits my face as I wait for his text messages. Who knew it could be this fun to tease him. I'm so lost in my own world messaging back and forth with Jay that I miss the blonde-haired woman scurrying past me. I try to grab her attention and rush after her but she storms into David's office and slams the door in my face.

I know I should've quit after the fiasco at my apartment but I was called in to a meeting with David and an HR rep where he apologized for his behavior in his office and very expertly avoided the topic of what happened in my apartment. He said that it would never happen again. And for some fucked up reason I agreed to stay on at my job.

Jay wasn't very happy about my decision (he did eventually find out that David is my boss), and every day since when five o'clock hits, there's a member of his team walking up to my desk and waiting for me to gather my stuff before escorting me downstairs and to my apartment. I don't care to fight him on it. It's better that he knows I am safe, and I also don't care to have my boss on the 6 p.m. news as a murder victim. Because if David touches me again, Jay will kill him. It isn't an idle threat.

Voices carry from inside and I know I shouldn't eavesdrop but I've never seen that woman in here before and she looked like she knew the place. Call it curiosity or whatever, but I press my ear up to his door.

"David," she almost sings as she strolls further into his office.

"Jane," David acknowledges her, his voice moving over to the far wall. "Drink?"

"No, gross. I don't know how you can stand that stuff."

"What can I help you with?"

"Why haven't you pulled the trigger yet?" She sounds impatient.

"Because I haven't."

"David, you know how Daddy gets when he doesn't get what he wants. And he wants her."

"I'm well aware of that, Jane."

I quickly glance over my shoulder and make sure that nobody is coming down the hall before pressing my ear back up to the door.

"Holy shit, you're falling for the little bitch."

He doesn't respond but I hear heels clicking on the floor and rustling.

"Honestly, Jane. I don't have time to deal with your bullshit right now. I have work to do."

"That's what you're calling them now? Your little conquests? Work?"

"What are you talking about?"

"The little brunette sitting out there. Seriously, David? In the office of all places."

My eyes widen at the realization that the only person they could be talking about is me. Now I'm not so sure if I should be eavesdropping but I can't seem to pull away now.

"Don't get too attached to her, David. Soon she'll just be another missing girl. And we'll be laying on a beach in Mexico."

"I'm not fucking falling for her. And it'll get done when it gets done. Now, get out, Jane."

"What? Why?"

"Because I have to get back to work and figure out how to not make all this fall back on this company."

Pushing away from the door I rush over to my desk and grab my purse and cellphone before hightailing it out of there. There's now no doubt in my mind that they were talking about me. But why? And what were they planning?

Soon she'll just be another missing girl.

Dry heaves rack my body as soon as I step out onto the

sidewalk and I have to throw my hand out against the wall of the building to keep myself from doubling over. My brain conjures up an image of the blonde-haired woman and David sitting around in his office with cocktails and discussing the best way to make me disappear. It makes my stomach roll.

A cab pulls up against the sidewalk in front of me and as soon as the couple get out I push past them and give the cab driver the address to a local pub. I don't even care that it's only two o'clock in the afternoon, right now Jose is calling my name and I'm about to answer with as many shots as I can consume until I either pass out or forget about what I heard in that office.

When I walk into the dimly lit pub I'm not expecting to see Jay sitting at the bar nursing a beer.

"Fancy meeting you here," I remark, placing my purse on the bar top and slipping onto the barstool next to him. I order a shot of tequila and a beer when the bartender comes to take my order.

"Hey, stranger." He nudges me with his elbow.

"Long day?" I ask tipping my chin at his beer.

"My job is made up of long days," he replies while watching me take the shot of tequila and suck on the lime. "Long day?"

"Don't want to talk about it." I hold up my shot glass to the bartender and he refills it.

"Ah, one of those days," he smirks, ordering two more shots.

"Yep," my lips make a popping sound with the word.

He and I go shot for shot until we're practically hanging off each other and the bartender eventually cuts us off. When my phone beeps for the tenth time since I entered the pub, he reaches over and snatches it up. I don't bother stopping him. We don't have any secrets between us.

His eyes harden when he sees the message. "He lay a hand on you again?"

He tries to raise an eyebrow but he fails miserably when both of his eyebrows rise at the same time. I can't help the laugh that breaks through, and he reaches out to grab my arm when I almost tip the barstool over.

"No. He wouldn't dare do that again," I laugh, not caring if everyone in the pub hears me. It's a nervous laugh though. When I'm steadier on the stool and feel confident enough that I'm not going to fall over again, I slap my hand on his back and lean into him. "You wanna know the funny thing? I got this vibe about him when I first started working there, like something wasn't quite right but I couldn't put my finger on it. Then he touched me. Twice." I jam a finger into my chest. "I ran out early today because I overheard him making plans to have me 'disappear'."

I shake my head and reach out to take another shot before realizing that the bartender has already cut us off. "I'm not even sure what that means, and I didn't stick around to find out because I'm not wearing underwear," I mumble, hanging my head.

He sputters and chokes next to me. "You what?"

A slow grin tugs at the corners of my mouth when I lift my eyes to his. "I'm not even wearing underwear. Have you not checked your pants pocket yet?"

Jay's face falls and his hands immediately go to searching the pockets of his tactical pants. His frantic search halts when his left hand slowly starts to pull out a piece of silk thong. "Jesus Christ. I've been walking around with these all day?" He throws some bills down on the bar and grabs my hand, pulling me behind him out of the pub. Instead of heading toward a waiting cab as I expect, Jay walks us back towards the Walker Advertising building

"Where are we going?"

"You're going to wait in the lobby while I go and have a little chat with your boss."

"Jay…"

My sentence is cut off when I see Parker, Mike, and a third equally menacing, step out of a blacked-out SUV.

When the hell did he text them?

"Cole," Jay barks at the third guy. "Stay down here with her. I don't want her upstairs while we're up there."

He nods. "Yes sir."

When Cole moves to stand next to me, even through my tequila-fogged brain I notice that his eyes are a unique shade of green.

Jay, Parker, and Mike were up there for a while before the elevator pings and the three of them walk out. Jay is wiping something off his knuckles with a paper towel.

Is that blood?

When they reach Cole and me, Jay nods towards the men and the three of them head off again. Jay doesn't say anything to me while he slips his arm around my waist and guides me into a nearby cab. Silence clouds us as the driver takes us closer towards my apartment.

"What happened?" My voice sounds small.

Jay runs a hand through his hair and blows out a breath. He doesn't say another word until we're pulling up to my apartment building and he's walking me to my door.

"What are we doing?" I press.

"You're not wearing panties," he growls.

"Jay – "

"No, Kat. You can't fucking say shit like that. I…fuck." He drops his head to his chest and runs another hand through his hair.

The look in his eyes when he lifts his head again has me backing up against my door but he follows, placing one hand above my head on the door and leaning in. His other hand grips my hip.

"What did you guys do up there?"

"You belong with me. You're mine, Kathrine. And I'll do whatever it takes to protect you," he whispers. "You said you overheard him talking about making you disappear. So, we questioned him, and that's all you need to know for now." His mouth is less than an inch away from mine.

Heat travels up my body and he groans when I bite my bottom lip between my teeth. Jay and tequila are a deadly combination. It's like wanting that last slice of chocolate cake but knowing that you'd have to run twenty extra miles on the treadmill tomorrow just to burn it off. But that damn chocolate cake keeps calling your name and you have to use all your willpower to resist the temptation. His mouth crashes down on mine, and all my willpower evaporates. I didn't have much willpower anyway.

I'm what you call a touchy-feely drunk, but most of the time I can still control my actions after a few shots. But not with Jay.

When I'm drunk on tequila shots and he's around, all my rules and inhibitions fly out the window. It's like tunnel vision takes over and the only thing I see is him. I can't get enough of him. At that point, he stops being my best friend and becomes the man I want to get lost in for a few hours.

He pulls away and leans his forehead against mine, our breathing heavy. "You're drunk," he breathes.

"So are you."

He shakes his head. "That's not what I meant. You only want me when you're drunk."

"And you're complaining? You're about to get laid."

"I want you to want me when you're sober."

I pull further away from him and lean my back against my apartment door. "Why? Why can't you just take what I'm giving you, Jay? This is all I have to give." My arms lift and then drop to my sides again.

He takes a step back shaking his head. He slips his hands into the front pockets of his jeans and eyes me with hurt swimming behind his intense stare.

"I don't believe that," he says and walks a few feet away before looking back over his shoulder. "You will be mine. The sooner you realize that, the better it'll be."

The minute the elevator doors close with him on the other side my phone pings with a new message.

David: Where are you?

Argh, not with you, asshole. Well, at least he's still alive.

What pisses me off the most is that Jay had a point.

He was right.

I did want him when I was drunk because I was too scared to admit how I felt when I was sober. Except for that one night in Toronto. But that's all we could have. One night.

8. MAKE ME FORGET

Jason

It's been four days since I kissed Kat outside of her apartment door and I know she's been avoiding me, ignoring my calls and texts. According to Alice, she also requested a few days off from the advertising company.

Well, I'm done beating around the bush. It's time to get everything out in the open. I knock on her apartment door and stick my hands in the front pockets of my jeans. I knock again when there's no answer.

"Come on Kat. I know you're in there. You can't ignore me forever."

The door swings open and she's leaning her hip against the entry way wall.

"I'm not ignoring you," she scowls.

"I think you are." I open the door wider and stroll into the apartment.

I grin when I notice all the cleaning supplies laying across the kitchen counter. Kat goes on a cleaning spree when she's mad, frustrated, or has a lot on her mind that she needs to think through.

From the looks of the supplies and the cleanliness of the apartment she's either extremely mad or has a shit ton on her mind. Everything in the kitchen and living room is spotless and gleaming and I bet if I go into all the bathrooms and bedrooms I'll find the same thing.

"What are you doing here, Jay" she sighs, throwing the rag in her hand into the bucket on the counter.

"We need to talk."

She glares up at me. "No, we don't."

Kat starts gathering up all the cleaning supplies and arranging them back into the storage bucket before placing them back under the sink.

I take a deep breath and start again, "Kat…"

"Jay, I don't want to ruin our friendship so if what you have to say has to do with you kissing me on Friday then you don't have to worry about it. We were drunk and it meant nothing. So, we're cool," she interrupts then smirks. "At least we didn't end up in bed together this time."

Enough of this.

I walk around the counter to where she's standing and block her in, her front to the counter and her back to my front. I run my hands down her waist and settle them at her hips.

"It meant nothing?" I whisper in her ear. I can see the small goose bumps appearing on her skin. I curl my fingers around her hips and dig them in slightly, bringing her against me as I lightly kiss the spot right under her ear. "It didn't mean nothing." I run my tongue down the slope of her neck and nip the top of her shoulder, my cock getting harder when I hear her sharp intake of breath.

"Jay..." it's barely more than whisper but it fans the fire already burning.

I spin her around and crush my mouth down on hers, tracing her bottom lip with my tongue as a plea for her to let me in. She opens slightly and I don't hesitate to explore the inside of her mouth. I groan, she tastes so good - like ripe strawberries. Her scent is intoxicating and I can't get enough of her green apple perfume. She smells and tastes like Katherine. My hands tangle in her hair as I angle her head to take the kiss deeper, willing her to touch me.

I don't have to wait long before her hands are running up my chest, one of them reaches up into my hair and her fingers grab hold and pull.

I run my other hand down lower over her back and cup her ass to pull her closer. Her hand on my chest starts venturing lower and lands on my cock. When she moans and starts stroking me through my jeans I think I'm going to come on the spot.

When I pull away, our breaths are heavy, panting. Kat's lips are swollen and she looks flushed. "Kat, I want you. I've wanted you for a while but if you're not ready I'll walk out that door."

She raises a disbelieving eyebrow and looks at me.

I grin. "I said I will, not that I would want to but I'll walk away for you, until you're-"

"Shut up," she cuts me off and reaches up on her tip toes pulling my mouth down to hers.

The kiss is hot and needy. My hands cup her ass and I lift her as her legs wrap around my waist and I walk us down the hall to her bedroom, pausing briefly to kick the door closed with the heel of my boot. Kat slides down my body and my cock jumps from the feel of her soft body pressed against my hard one. My thumbs lightly skim up her sides as I move her t-shirt up and over her head and drop it next to us, her pants soon join it on the floor. I can't help but stare at her, her bra and panties the only thing preventing me from seeing all of her.

My eyes trail their way up from her black booty shorts, over her flat stomach, her full breasts, and finally land on her amber eyes burning with need.

"Kat, you need to stop looking at me like that or I'm not going to last," I growl, starting toward her as a deep blush creeps up her face.

Katherine

After removing my bra, Jay lays me gently down on the bed and moves away. I lean up on my elbows needing to feel his body back on mine, when I see that he's already taken off his shirt and has his jeans and boxers half way down his legs. I feel my breath hitch when he stands up tall again and I have to remind myself not to drool.

I'm fully aware that I've already seen him naked *but holy crap, Batman*. The guy is built; I don't even think there's an ounce of fat on him anywhere.

The bed dips under his weight when he crawls back up my body and settles on top of me capturing my lips with his again. His one hand trails down my side before stopping under my thigh and hitching my leg around his waist. My fingers roam over his back and I moan when I feel his cock press even more against my still panty-clad clit. His lips find that sensitive spot just under my ear again and my body becomes a ticking time bomb ready to explode. I need him in me now.

Apparently, he is in the business of reading minds because not even a minute later he sits back on his knees and lifts both of my legs so that my toes are pointing to the ceiling. He slowly thumbs off my panties.

Bastard is enjoying torturing me slowly.

After he discards my booty shorts by throwing them over his shoulder, he runs both hands down the outside of my legs, before trailing the fingers of one hand back up to hold my ankles together while the other skims over my pussy lips. A moan escapes my mouth when he pushes a finger inside of me.

"God, you're so wet." He groans, adding a second finger and pumping in and out of me.

Oh, fuck. I think I'm going to come.

The angle is so intense that I'm already looking over the edge of no return. Just when I think I'm going to tumble over, he removes his fingers and I feel the bed dip again when he gets up to grab a condom and comes back already rolling it on.

I'm going insane and if he doesn't get his cock inside of me soon there may be a murder; I'm not even kidding. But thank god, he doesn't take long. His one hand grabs my ankles again holding them up while his other hand strokes his cock and he lines up with my pussy.

"Be mine," he growls, sliding into me an inch.

When I shake my head, he withdraws the head of his dick.

"Be mine," he repeats, sliding slowly into me but not giving me his full length.

When I shake my head again, he withdraws until his dick is

almost fully out.

"Jay," I groan. He's torturing me slowly.

"Be mine, Katherine." He slowly pushes into me again.

"Okay," I pant, my back arching when he slams his full length into me.

Holy fuck, that feels so good.

When he's in all the way, he let's go of my ankles and my legs fall over each of shoulders. He pumps into me with short, even strokes at first but then gets harder and faster. It takes everything I have in me to not scream every time he hits that sweet spot.

"Don't stop," I moan.

"Never," he responds.

He drops one of my legs from his shoulders and instead places it around his waist changing the angle again

"Ah, fuck. I'm going to come."

"Come for me, baby," he growls in my ear.

And just like that I feel wave after wave of my orgasm crash through me as he still pumps into me a few more times before I feel him stiffen and groan with his own release.

Eventually he pulls out, leaving me longing to feel him inside me again. My legs are like jelly when he collapses next to me and I finally lower them back down to the bed. They're going to fucking hurt in the morning but it will have been worth it.

Who needs leg day at the gym when you can have sex like that?

He goes to my bathroom to dispose of the condom and clean himself up before bringing me back a warm cloth and cleaning me up too. He tosses the cloth on the floor among our discarded clothes and climbs into bed bringing the covers up and over us before pulling my back against his front and settling his arm around my middle. Unaware of the clusterfuck that my life is about to become, I snuggle closer into him, wiggling my ass and earning a groan out of him as I smile to myself before drifting off to sleep.

9. MY WAY

Jason

Morning light streams through the open curtains of Kat's bedroom windows and I groan as I turn my head to see the time on my phone read 7 a.m. If my body would cooperate I could get at least another two hours of sleep in before the alarm goes off but there's a fat chance of that happening. I haven't slept passed seven in what feels like years.

The smell of bacon and freshly brewed coffee invade my senses around the same time I realize that Kat is no longer sleeping beside me.

I'm just pulling up my jeans over my boxers when her phone pings from atop of her nightstand across the room.

David: Need you to accompany me to a business dinner tonight.

My skin prickles with anger and frustration. After pulling my shirt over my head, I head out to find her in the kitchen standing over a pan of sizzling bacon.

"Coffee's ready," she throws over her shoulder.

I don't say anything while I grab a cup and add cream. I try to act casual when I take a seat at the counter and place her phone face up on the counter top.

"David texted you."

Her back straightens and her shoulders square when I mention his name. For a minute, I think she's not going to face me, that maybe she'll just pretend not to have heard me and carry on with making breakfast. But then she looks up at me, uncertainty in her eyes.

"It's a business dinner."

"Kat." My voice comes out sounding as more of a warning than I wanted.

Her body stiffens when I move from my seat and walk towards her as I watch all the emotions flash across her eyes and play out on her face: fear, uncertainty, and lastly, regret.

"Jay, I – "

"You're going back to work for him," I guess correctly.

"I-I..." she drops her head, "Yes."

My thumb gently caresses her cheek. "Don't."

She pushes my hand away and steps around me, walking out of the kitchen and into her living room before spinning around to face me. "It was a mistake leaving the office like I did the other day. I don't even know what I overheard. It could be nothing." She pauses, her hand motioning between us. "And this...was a mistake too."

"This wasn't a mistake," I refute.

Kat crosses her arms over her chest and I recognize it as the same move she does when the walls around her slam shut. I've seen that look a thousand times but it was never directed at me. Before now.

"He tried to hurt you, Kat."

She shakes her head then shrugs her shoulders. "And he apologized. HR seems to think it won't happen again."

"I don't buy it." I try to move toward her but for every step forward I take, she takes one back.

"Jay, this job means a lot to me. I'm not even sure of what I overheard in his office, and HR already knows about the assault. I would just like to move on from all of this."

When tears start pooling in her eyes and she refuses to meet my gaze, I retreat, grabbing my leather jacket from the back of her couch and my helmet from her coffee table.

"Jason," I hear her whisper behind me when I reach the front door.

"If he hurts you again I'll kill him," I state before closing the door behind me and jumping on my Ducati.

Twenty minutes later I'm parking my bike next to Parker's identical one in Mike's driveway.

"Hey! Didn't think you were coming," Mike comments when I walk into his kitchen.

"Change of plans," I reply, opening the fridge and grabbing a bottle of Heineken. I down the contents of the bottle and pop open another one before turning to them.

When I look up, Parker has an eyebrow raised but doesn't say anything. Thank god. The last thing I need is the two of them throwing questions at me about Kat.

"You guys want to head to Gotcha's tonight?" I ask, raising the bottle to my lips.

"Mark and Cole were already heading there tonight. I'll let them know we'll meet them," Mike responds, pulling out his phone.

Mark and Cole are also part of our Emergency Response Teams, and the only two the three of us have hung out with outside of work in the last year.

"You in?" I tip my chin towards Parker.

"Dani and I have a babysitter for tonight. It's date night," Parker responds taking another mouthful of his beer. "But she might want to go out after dinner," he adds.

I nod and finish my beer. "I'm heading to the range for a bit. Got a new assault rifle calling my name." Grabbing my keys, I go to make my way back to the front door when Mike yells from behind me.

"Dude, what the fuck? Did you just come to drink my beer?"

I can't help the chuckle that escapes. It shouldn't be this fun to fuck with him. "It was good beer."

Parker's laugh from the kitchen only makes me want to laugh harder. The three of us have known each other since kindergarten and Mike has always been the one to get riled up so damn easily. He's always been the hot-headed one. It doesn't matter where we are, he somehow manages to get into an argument with somebody. Case in point, when Parker was in the hospital and Dani's psycho ex kidnapped her, Mike got into an argument with Alice over an action film.

Yup, you heard that right folks - an action film!

But he and Parker are like brothers to me, so it's my duty as the oldest one to press as many of their buttons as possible. I'm afraid that Mike might break a tooth with the way his jaw is clenched right now so I throw my hands up. "Relax, don't get your panties in a wad. First round's on me tonight."

He doesn't respond, just turns back to the kitchen where Parker is still laughing.

I'm just about to load a new clip into the new 9mm I purchased when I hear her walk up behind me. I know it's her because she's the only one I've brought up here.

"Shouldn't you be at a dinner date?"

"It's a business dinner, and that's not til later."

I can tell she's hesitant to come any closer when I have the gun in my hand, so I slip the safety on and holster it before turning my full attention to her.

"Jay…" she starts but I cut her off.

"You don't have to explain."

"You scare me," she blurts out and then hurries to explain when she sees the hurt and confused look on my face. "This scares me," she gestures between the two of us.

"Kat –"

"You're my best friend, Jason. I don't think I could forgive myself if anything happened and I lost you."

I'm unable to stop myself anymore. I walk over to her, place my palms on either side of her face and kiss her. I kiss her like my life depends on it. I put everything into the kiss and when we finally pull apart, our breaths are heavy and her lips are swollen.

"You could never lose me." I rest my forehead against hers and just stare into her amber eyes.

Her hands come up to grip my wrists, gently tugging my hands away from her face as she takes a step back, a tear rolling down her face.

"I can't do this. I'm sorry, Jason." Her eyes hesitantly look up at mine before she turns and bolts back the way she came.

"Fuck!"

Foregoing the 9mm, I reach down and pick up the new assault rifle I'm supposed to be trying out for the team.

Katherine

The club is packed when we arrive, which really shouldn't shock me as much as it does. It's one of the few clubs in this city that plays good music. I love the DJ here. The music he plays is easy to let myself get lost in and that's exactly what I need right now.

The "business dinner" with David turned out to be just dinner. There was no business involved. He lied to lure me into meeting him. As soon as I found out that there wasn't a business aspect to it, I turned around and left. I never even sat down.

I missed Jay, even though I had seen him early today. I missed his touch. I missed hearing his voice. Hearing his voice was like sipping a fine wine in a hot bubble bath after a long day. But it was more than that. So much more than that. I could lay in a dark room for hours and just let the sound of his voice wash over me. It's authoritative, demanding, and yet extremely arousing. And as much as I said that whatever was happening between us was a mistake, it wasn't.

But there was no way that we could be together.

Jason wanted a family, he wanted to marry the perfect girl and have kids. And I...I just couldn't be that for him. I didn't want kids. I didn't want to chance that I would turn out exactly like my mother; I could never subject a child to that abuse. So as much as it sucked to hurt him like I know I did, I needed to keep it strictly friends between us.

Or I could be overthinking things again and getting way too deep inside my own head. I'm supposed to be enjoying the night. As soon as I left the restaurant, I called Alice and she insisted that I come out with her tonight. Not wanting to waste a decent outfit, I agreed.

"Come on, first round is on me," Alice yells over the music, grabbing my hand and leading us around the crowded dance floor and over to the bar.

"No tequila," I try to yell back but she doesn't hear me or she's choosing to ignore me because the next thing I know the bartender is placing a bowl of limes in front of us, a salt shaker, and two shots of tequila. "Alice…" I groan.

"Oh, come on. One tequila shot won't kill you. And plus, Jason's not here so you're in the clear," she smirks before licking the salt off the top of her hand and slamming back the shot.

She's got a point. Jason isn't here so I should be okay. As long as she does her best friend duty and doesn't let me around any hot guy. Just as I pop the lime in my mouth after slamming back my own shot, a tall figure walks up and stops in the middle of Alice and me.

Ah, fuck.

"Fancy seeing you ladies here," Mike grins. Jason is behind him.

"Buy a girl a drink?" Alice bats her eyelashes at Mike and runs one dark painted finger nail down the center of his chest. It's almost comical the way Mike puffs out his chest when she does that. But he doesn't hesitate to pull out his wallet and throw a fifty on the bar motioning to the bartender for six more shots.

"Um, I'm good," I stammer looking from Jay to Alice.

"Just one shot," Alice pouts, handing me another shot from the ones the bartender just poured.

"Fine," I sigh taking the shot from her, "but you better pull best friend duty," I add.

"Deal," Alice grins just as Parker and Danielle walk up and Mike hands them their shots.

I've already got a good buzz going on after that second shot when Alice grabs Danielle and me by the hand and leads us onto the dance floor just as the DJ plays the Tiesto remix of Calvin

Harris' "My Way." It doesn't take long for the beat to take over my body; it never does when it comes to Calvin Harris.

This right here, dancing like no one is watching with my two best girlfriends, is what I needed. Except, that's total bullshit because someone is watching. And his intense emerald eyes on me makes me want to roll my hips a little slower and dip a little lower.

And then the shame and the guilt set in, making my feet falter. I know I shouldn't be teasing him like this especially after my whole speech about wanting to keep it strictly friends.

"I'm going to get some fresh air," I yell in Alice's ear.

Jason

Watching the way Kat slowly rolls her hips from side to side is driving me fucking crazy. All I can think of is the way those hips bucked when she came undone under me, and the way she moaned my name in that melodious voice.

I know I shouldn't follow her outside but I can't help it. I'm fucking drawn to this woman. There may as well be a magnetic pull drawing us together. As much I'd like to, I can't get her out of my head.

When I make it outside, Kat is holding up the brick wall with her back, her head leaning back against it. Her arms are wrapped around her middle and her breathing is heavy.

Every protective instinct in my body goes on high alert at the sight. But as soon as she turns her head and sees me, she immediately drops her arms and straightens away from the wall.

"You okay?" I ask, slowly approaching her.

"Why wouldn't I be?"

"Kat, you can cut the façade. You forget that I know you better than anyone else." I prop one booted foot up against the same wall and lean my upper back against it and wait her out.

It doesn't take long.

"I'm sorry, Jay," she sighs leaning back against the wall next to me.

"For what?"

"For this back and forth bullshit. For ruining our friendship."

I straighten off the wall and turn towards her. There's guilt and regret swimming behind those amber eyes but the instant my eyes connect with hers I know what I need to do.

I should never have made her feel like I wanted more or nothing at all. Now I see that if I really love her the way I'm convinced I do then I have to step away and let her be happy, even if that happiness is not with me.

If you love something set it free, and all that bullshit.

I reach out and curl my hand around the back of her neck, caressing the side of her face with my thumb. "You didn't ruin our friendship, Kat. And I'm the one who needs to apologize."

Her fingers wrap around my hand on her neck as she looks up at me. "Jay…"

I shake my head but refuse to drop my hand just yet. "I'm taking a step back, Kat. I'll go back to being the best friend and I'll support you in whatever you need. This is what I should've done from the beginning but I was selfish. I wanted you to myself. But I'd rather have you in my life as a friend than not have you at all. Just answer me one thing."

"Okay."

"Are you happy?"

There's a saying that says that the eyes are the windows to the soul, that all of what we're feeling and thinking can be seen reflected in them. There's so much expression in the eyes and each are unique to the individual. I always believed that when it came to Katherine. From the minute we met, I could tell what she was feeling or thinking from the way her eyes would change color. This time isn't any different. When she answered that she is happy, I know she is lying. What I see behind those eyes is the opposite of wanting to keep things friendly. But I already agreed to take a step back so I will.

But if I am going to give her up then I am going to give us one more night for the memory banks. "Come on. They're playing our song." I slip my hand in hers and tug her towards me.

Katherine

He's staring at my lips when I finally get up the courage to look at him. His emerald eyes darken when his hand runs up my inner thigh and goose bumps appear all over my skin. My breath hitches when he leans in, his hand leaving my thigh and cupping my neck.

The alcohol from the tequila makes my head buzz and my skin heat when he's close enough I can feel his breath on my lips. But he doesn't move any closer. He pauses, his eyes searching mine for any reason why he shouldn't continue this.

I want to tell him that we shouldn't cross this line again, but to hell with it. I want him. I wanted to jump him when we were standing outside of the club and he asked me if I was happy. Then I wanted to jump him again in the cab ride over to my place. He was only supposed to drop me off, but he somehow ended up coming inside with me.

This man is just too intoxicating and I can't deny that I want to taste him tonight, even if it means beating myself up about it tomorrow.

When he realizes that I'm not going to tell him no, his lips brush mine. His tongue traces the seam between my top and bottom lip and I open for him.

The kiss is soft at first but gets hotter and demanding the longer our lips are locked. He lays me down on the couch and his body towers over mine. With one hand, he explores every inch of my body he can reach while leaning on his other forearm keeping himself from overwhelming me with his weight.

My legs instinctively wrap around his waist and my hips lift trying to create more friction. I moan when I feel him already hard behind his zipper.

His hand caresses down my side to the hem of my skirt where it slips under and moves up to squeeze my ass cheek, lifting me higher. I am so very grateful that I had chosen to wear my new sapphire blue satin thong and matching bra today rather than the old mismatched sets I usually wear.

Gentlemen, if the woman you're about to sleep with is wearing matching underwear. You weren't the one who decided to get laid. Just saying, she probably had it already planned.

However, in this case. I really wasn't planning on this. I was just really excited to break out my new Victoria's Secret underwear and no lines showed under the skirt I had chosen to wear. It was either that or go commando.

Going commando was only hot when you were trying to torture the man you're with with images of sex and to watch him squirm for hours until he's able to get home to you.

His fingers dip beneath my thong and all thoughts leave when he starts rubbing circles on my clit. The back of my head pushes into the arm of the couch, and my back arches up in an attempt to get closer to the edge. I know I'm not going to last long, especially if he keeps up this steady assault of his mouth on my skin and fingers on my clit.

"Jesus, I'm going to come just from hearing you moan like that," he breathes in my ear.

And that's all I need to tumble over the edge. I come hard, squeezing my legs closed around his hand and my eyes shut. I don't open them until I hear him chuckle.

"What?" I can feel my cheeks start to heat.

"You're sexy when you come." He moves to let me up.

"Do you want me to, um, you know?" I raise an eyebrow and glance at the impressive bulge in his pants.

Jay grins, places a kiss on my forehead and then leaves. Leaving me standing in the middle of my living room utterly confused, and drunk.

"No, no, no."

This can't be happening. It's a dream. It has to be. I'm going to wake up in my bed and it would've all just been dream.

But as I stare down at the two pink little lines, I know it's not a dream. Two pink and blue lines stare up at me from seven different pregnancy tests.

Seven.

I figured there was something wrong with the first one, so I rushed out to the drug store down the street and bought six more. But they all say what I've been trying to avoid.

Pregnant.

I'm pregnant with my best friend's baby.

10. PROPOSITION

Jason

The next morning when I walk into the office, I'm cursing myself and Fireball Whisky. Mike insisted on buying everyone a couple rounds and since we're all suckers for free liquor we obliged him in his sick game. Everything is a little too loud and a little too bright this morning.

"You look like shit," Parker comments when I make a beeline for the coffee maker.

"Thanks, asshole," I reply right before bringing the coffee mug to my lips and tasting the sweet heaven that is caffeine. "Please tell me we don't have to leave the office today and my hungover ass can just sit in that chair all day."

Parker laughs, "No can do, Miller. The drug unit might need our help today."

"Fucking seriously?" I bark and instantly wince.

Damn hangover.

I was okay with maybe going out if homicide needed our help but if the drug unit has come a-calling that means I will need to do shit.

Like raid a fucking building. Hungover.

"Yeah. Apparently, they're planning on taking down a dealer they've been after for months."

"The information you requested the other day just came in," Mark says, handing me a folder stacked full.

"What's that?" Parker asks as I'm scanning down the front page.

"I had Mark get his friend to look into David Walker for me."

"Why couldn't you have done that?" Parker questions.

"Err, because the information I want goes beyond our database."

"So, what does it say?" Mike inquires, grabbing his own coffee cup.

"You guys ever hear of the Knights MC in Ontario?"

All three of them shake their heads when Parker reaches for the file and I hand it over.

"Suspected in drug, weapons, and human trafficking," he reads.

"You're telling me this Walker guy is associated with the MC?" Mike asks, filling his cup.

"Not him. But his wife, Jane Walker, is the step-daughter of the president of the club."

"Shit. So what Kat overheard could be legit," Mark contemplates.

"What now?" Mike inquires, taking another sip of his coffee.

"Cole," I yell out to the hall, wincing again at how loud my voice sounds, but feeling a little better when I notice Parker and Mike doing the same.

"Yes, sir?"

"Get me everything you can on everyone David Walker's been in contact with over the last couple years, including phone records."

"You really think that's necessary, Jay?" Parker asks skeptically.

"If he's somehow involved in their human trafficking ring, I need to make sure that Kat isn't on their radar."

"Well, then let's pay a visit to David Walker," Parker suggests.

"How may I help you, gentlemen? Gail said you were from the RCMP?" He rises to shake hands with Parker, Mike, and me before reclaiming his seat behind his desk.

Of course, he doesn't recognize us. The last time we came face to face in his office his eyes were almost swollen shut. And the first time we met in Kat's apartment he was more worried about getting blood on his expensive clothes than on the person who broke his nose.

"Yes, sir. We just have some questions about your wife, Jane," Parker says taking a seat in one of the leather chairs in front of Walker's desk. "We have some questions for her regarding a case, but we can't seem to get a hold of her."

While Parker talks with Walker, Mike roams around the large office. To anyone outside of the special ops teams, it might look like he's just taking in everything, maybe looking for something that doesn't fit. And while that's part of it, the other part is he's subtly positioning himself on the other side of the office behind David in case the fucker gets any bright ideas.

"Questions about a case?"

"A trafficking case," I clarify, and watch as the blood drains from his face.

As I look up from my desk, I see my old CO stepping off the elevator.

"Miller!" His voice booms from out in the hallway.

Despite having been out of the military for almost six years his voice still makes me snap to attention. It's one of those voices that commands attention wherever he goes; it makes you want to listen to what he's got to say.

He's still in extremely decent shape for someone approaching his sixties. Back when I was still on his spec ops team, the guy could run circles around us, and our team was the best of the best. I'm almost positive that he still could.

"Smith."

He laughs extending his hand to me, "You're not part of my team anymore, Jason. You don't have to call me CO or Smith."

"Sorry, sir. It's a habit," I respond, taking my hand back.

"You can drop the sir too. It's just Tyler."

"What can I do for you, Tyler?"

"Can we step into your office for a minute?" He asks signaling back towards the door I just came out of, and leading the way.

When we enter my office, I take a seat back behind my desk as

Tyler closes the door behind us before taking up the seat on the other side.

"I have a proposition for you, Jason."

"Sir?"

"I'd like you to rejoin the old team. The new guys coming in don't have what it takes to survive out there right now and I need someone to whip them into shape."

"Neither did we but you changed that," I smirk remembering the countless hours spent training.

Smith leans forward resting his elbows on his knees. "I'm retiring in a few years. I know it's early but I've been at this a long time and Mae and I are ready to settle somewhere tropical and enjoy the rest of our lives with our grandkids. I'd like to be able to refer you for the job when I leave."

"Sir?" I hear what he's saying but I'm having a hard time processing it.

"If you re-enlist and agree to rejoin the old team I'll be recommending you for CO when I retire," he confirms.

I stare at him with utter disbelief on my face. On the one hand, it would be an honor to take over once he leaves, but on the other hand, those are some big fucking shoes to fill and I'm not sure I would be up for the challenge.

"I'll give you some time to think it over. But you should know that the lieutenant already approves of my decision and Max and Drake have agreed to re-enlist right along with you."

"Sounds like it really would be the old team together again."

"With the three of you back, it would be the entire team back together," he amends.

I knew that Max and Drake got out shortly after I did but I had no idea that the rest of the team had stayed. Which just reminds me of how miserably I failed at keeping in contact with the men I used to call my brothers.

"Think about it," Smith says, getting up and moving towards the door. "Oh, and I was under strict orders from Mae not to leave until you agreed to come for dinner one night this week."

I lean back in my chair placing a hand over my flat stomach, "I don't know if my closet could handle one of Mae's dinners. Seriously, that woman is a pro in the kitchen."

Smith laughs patting his own stomach. "Boy, why do you think I work out as much as I do. I swear that woman is trying to make me fat in my old age."

While we wait for the elevator, he reaches out and pats me on the back. "I mean it, Miller. Think about re-enlisting and let me know."

"Yes, Sir."

Smith laughs as he steps on when the doors open. "Again with the sir."

"Old habits die hard," I grin.

He chuckles shaking his head. "Next Sunday, 6 p.m. for dinner," he adds before the doors close and the elevator descends taking him back down to the lobby.

"Jason," Cole calls as he walks towards me. "I was able to get in touch with an old friend. He's deep undercover but wants to meet you," he adds, handing me a fax print out.

"Run it by Parker first, then make it happen."

"I did it!" Kat squeals when she spots me in the parking lot.

Today was the last day of her restricted gun licensing class.

"Congrats," I laugh and catch her when she throws her arms around my neck.

"So I can take my gun home now?" she inquires, pulling away and bouncing on the balls of her feet. She looks like a kid who was left in a candy store and told that they could have anything they want.

"Sure," I chuckle, opening the passenger side door for her. A wide smile appears on her face as she hops up and into the cab of the truck.

When I'm settled behind the wheel, I grin as I turn toward her. "Your gun is at my house but we have to make a stop first."

"Okay…where are we stopping?"

I try to keep a straight face as I maneuver us into traffic. "My former CO and his wife invited me over for dinner tonight. I don't have time to drop you off before heading over there so…"

"Wait. Your CO? As in your Commanding Officer from the military?"

"That's the one."

"Jay…" her eyes go wide and she crosses her arms in disbelief. "I'm not going to dinner with your CO," she says, shaking her head.

"Well, it's too late because we're here." I grin as I place the truck in park.

Her head snaps to the right to look out the window before she slowly turns back to me, narrowing her eyes. "You owe me."

Mae answers the door when I ring the doorbell. You'd never guess that she'll be celebrating her fifty-eighth birthday in just a few months; she doesn't look a day over forty.

"Well, hi, stranger," she greets me with a wide smile on her face.

"Mae," I lean down, placing a peck on her cheek like I've always done since shortly after meeting her.

"Jason Miller, it's about time you showed your face around here again," she teases.

"I was told I didn't have much of a choice," I grin.

Mae grins, patting my shoulder. Then her gaze lands on Kat and her grin gets wider. "Excuse my manners. Mae Smith," she offers as she holds her hand out to Kat.

"Kat," she says, placing her hand in Mae's. Her eyes go wide when Mae uses that as an opportunity to pull her into a hug. I can't hold back the chuckle that escapes my throat at Kat's reaction.

"Jason, why don't you go find Tyler while the girls go chat in the kitchen. I think you'll find him in his office."

I'm not sure which is more amusing, Kat's expression when Mae insisted on hugging her, or her expression when Mae pretty much pulls her in the direction of the kitchen without much choice. Her amber eyes go wide in shock and plead with me to help her as she is dragged away.

I should not be enjoying it this much.

When I poke my head around the door to the CO's office, he's standing in front of the floor-to-ceiling window looking lost in thought, a scotch in one hand, the other in the front pocket of his dress pants.

"Sir."

"Well, look what the cat dragged in," he jokes, turning slightly from the window.

I always loved the view from his office. He and Mae live far enough away that the city doesn't reach here. On a clear night you have an uninterrupted view of the night sky. "Have you given any more thought to my proposition?"

"Not yet, sir. My team just came across a case that I'd like to see through to the end."

He nods. "I'll need an answer either way by this time next month."

"Yes, sir."

"Come on," he says as he places his scotch glass down on his desk, then slaps me on my back. "Let's go eat."

11. WALK AWAY

Jason

My phone rings for the third time since I've been sparring in the ring with Parker. I have a feeling I already know who it is. I promised my old CO that I would have a decision on whether I will be rejoining my old team or not by the end of today. But I just can't bring myself to make the call.

Or to answer his.

I do miss it. The action. Fighting to defend our country. The brotherhood. But I'm not entirely sure I want to leave the Emergency Response Team yet. Or Katherine.

When my phone rings for the fourth time, Parker stops and throws his hands up.

"For the love of god, just answer your damn phone, man."

"I haven't made a decision yet. If I answer it, he's going to want an answer right away."

"Just tell him to give you another twenty-four hours. He's waited this long. Another day won't kill him." Parker throws his gloves on the bench before grabbing his water bottle.

When I reach for my phone, it's not the CO's number I see on the call display.

"Is this Jason Miller?" an older tiny female voice asks.

"It is."

"I'm Kat's neighbor. She gave me this number when she first moved in and told me that if I ever noticed anything suspicious to give you a call."

"All right, is there something I can help you with, Mrs....?"

"Watts. I got home a couple minutes ago and there were sounds coming from her apartment."

Kat had told me about her. She said she was a sweet elderly woman but barely left her apartment or got any visitors. Kat said it seemed as if she was the only one who bothered to pay any attention to the woman, and Kat was fairly certain that if she never brought her groceries she wouldn't be eating either.

"What kind of sounds?"

"Screams," she whispers.

My back straightens with her explanation.

"I'll be there soon. Don't open the door for anyone," I say into the receiver before hanging up.

"What was that about?" Parker asks from the bench.

"Kat's neighbor says she heard screams coming from Kat's apartment." I throw over my shoulder while stuffing my boxing gloves back into my gym bag.

"I'll call the teams in."

"No, we don't know what we're dealing with yet. I'd rather not call in all three teams if we don't need the manpower. Just call in Mike, Cole, and Mark. Tell them to meet us outside of the apartment building."

He nods already dialing.

Parker, acting as my second, gives me the signal and I waste no time in kicking down the door to Kat's apartment.

When we arrived, there was no mistaking the sounds her neighbor was hearing. They were Kat's ear piercing screams and I would have bet anything that I knew who was the cause of those screams.

The scene that greets me when we storm into the apartment is one I'll never forget. David is laying on top of a naked Kat on the floor in her living room, with a knife to her throat and is in the process of getting his pants undone.

"You sonofabitch!"

His head snaps up at the snarl in my voice, as if the door being kicked down wasn't loud enough for him to hear.

"Ah, Jason. Just in time to watch the show."

I go to take a step forward but Kat screams and David shakes his head.

106

"I wouldn't if I were you. One more step and I'll slit her throat."

David hasn't caught Cole and Mike slowly making their way closer to him yet, waiting for me to give them the signal to take him out.

I hold my hands up. "What was your plan here, David? To rape and kill her, and what? Pray that I didn't find out and hunt your sorry-excuse-for-a-man ass down? That I wouldn't kill you as soon as you make that slice? That I won't kill you right now?"

David chuckles. "For once, you don't have the upper hand here, Jason. I think I'll enjoy the fact that I'll force you to watch while I take what's supposed to be mine, while I slide my cock inside her sweet, warm pussy, while I fuck her better than you ever could. And then when I slide my blade along this delicate flesh of hers."

What happens next goes by in a blur. I don't remember if I did give Cole and Mike the signal but when I blink again David is passed out on the floor and Katherine is in my arms. Shaking, but in my arms.

"Put him in my truck and I'll meet you at the warehouse."

Kat's grip on the back of my shirt tightens when I try to move away from her. Parker, Mike, Cole, and Mark nod their understanding and quietly slip from the apartment with David in hand.

"Don't leave me alone again," she sobs into my chest.

I'm trying my best to comfort her but I need to know. "Kat, was David...was he able to..."

Her face lifts as new tears pool in her eyes but she shakes her head. "No, you got here just in time."

"Thank Christ." I kiss the top of her head and tighten my arms around her, savoring the way she fits against me. She's safe and that's all I care about but when I'm done here, that fucker's going to pay.

While Kat is having a bath and changing into more comfortable clothes, I make a quick phone call, hopeful when they assure me they'll be here as soon as they can. It seems that Parker may have already beat me to calling them. My next phone call is to have her door repaired.

She's almost fully asleep in my arms when her front door quietly opens again. She jumps when she hears footsteps.

"It's okay. It's just Dani and Alice," I soothe her, placing a soft kiss on her head.

"You said you weren't going to leave me again," her voice is small, panicked.

"I know, and I'll come right back. But there's something I need to take care of real quick. If anything happens just stick Alice on them. She'll scare anyone away."

"Hey!" Alice pretends to pout and then laughs which earns a small grin from Kat.

"You'll come straight back?"

I nod. "I promise."

"Okay."

"We'll take care of her," Dani chimes in while I untangle myself from Kat.

The funny thing is, out of these girls, Alice is the one who I know would be able to handle anyone who comes through this door. I'm not saying that Dani and Kat wouldn't, but Alice is tough, she's fearless, and she could make a grown man piss his pants.

"Damnit, Jay. You didn't kill him, did you?" Parker asks when I open the truck bed and David's still form comes into view. Whoever knocked him out must've knocked him out good. The guy hasn't moved since Kat's apartment.

Cole leans over pressing two fingers to the inside of David's neck. "He's alive."

"Fucking hell, Jay," Parker sighs. "You're not going to kill him."

"Relax," I say, throwing his limp body over my shoulder in a fireman's hold. "I won't fully kill him. Maybe just beat him within an inch of his life."

When Parker realizes that I'm not budging on the issue he drops his head and walks ahead to unlock the door. "We'll fuck with his head a bit but that's it, Jay."

Mike snorts behind me while the other two chuckle.

Yeah, laugh it up, boys.

The truth is, these three men know me too well. If someone has the audacity to fuck with someone I care about, I'm not going to sit idly by and watch it happen. Just like when Adam fucked with Danielle and Parker went ape shit about hunting him down and killing him. Parker put a single bullet right between his eyes. I'm not saying I'm going to kill this asshole but by the time I'm done, he's going to know to not take any threat I utter lightly.

He sexually assaulted her, not once, but three times. If it were up to me I would've done this after the first time. But I had strict orders from our Inspector to make sure David lived. Now, I'm not following orders and it'll probably get me kicked from the teams but I don't give a fuck. The son-of-a-bitch almost raped Kat twice and came closer to killing her this last time. That doesn't fly with me. He isn't a man, he is scum. By the time I'm done with him, sitting on a beach will be the last thing on his mind.

Mark drags a chair to the middle of the room and I flop David onto it, binding his hands behind the back of the chair.

"Oh, for fuck's sake," Parker exclaims when I slip my fingers through the brass knuckles I pulled from my pants pocket.

I turn my cold eyes on Parker. "I backed you when you went after Adam after what he did to Danielle. It's now your turn to have my back. So are you with me on this or not?"

Mike sighs, "he's got a point, man."

Parker takes the water bottle Cole hands him. "Let's just get this over with. Danielle's ovulating and I was supposed to be home twenty minutes ago."

Cole laughs, "That's why he's in such a pissy mood. He's supposed to be getting some love from his woman."

Parker glares at Cole. "Just wait until you get married, asshole. You won't be laughing then."

I swear Cole and Mike are about to bust a gut with the way they're laughing but I'm over the back and forth banter now. I'm ready to wake this fucker up and teach him a lesson.

"Ready?" I look to Parker who's unscrewing the cap on the water bottle.

"Rise and shine princess," he says dumping the entire bottle in David's face.

12. TIME
Katherine

I haven't told Jason about the pregnancy and I never wished that he were here with me more than I do right now. I know he left last night to deal with David, and I was okay with that. Before, it would've bugged me when he used violence to deal with violence, but in this case, I could care less what happened to David. My give-a-fuck meter was low. He must have come back really late because he wasn't here when I eventually went to bed, but when I tried to roll over in the middle of the night, I rolled right into him and that gloriously naked chest of his.

"Good morning, beautiful."

I love the sound of his voice in the morning, it's husky and sexy as fuck.

"Good morning," I smile into his side.

"Coffee?"

"Hmm, tea for me, please."

Jay raises a questioning eyebrow. "You never drink tea. You okay?"

"Yeah, just trying to cut down on my caffeine consumption," I say dismissively while getting up and making my way to the attached bathroom.

When I come out, Jay is busy making us breakfast. Shirtless.

Oh, be still my racing heart.

Just as my eyes trace down the narrowing of his back to his hips, I notice a piece of paper sticking out from his back pocket.

"What's in your pocket?" I ask, my curiosity getting the better of me.

Jay turns, a playful smirk on his face and I can see in his eyes that he's battling with himself not to turn my question into a dirty joke. He surprises me when he moves closer, his thumb gently stroking the side of my face, his forehead resting on mine.

"Give us a chance, Kat. I know I'm not rich and I can't ever promise you fancy houses and cars, or expensive vacations. But I can promise to give you all of me. I can promise to love you like no one ever could. Just…give me a chance."

Tears flow down my face as I slowly shake my head. Regret instantly floods my body. I wish I could just tell him the truth. I would choose him in a heartbeat.

If only that choice was mine to make.

His shoulders drop in defeat as his hand slips from my face and goes to pull the piece of paper from the back pocket of his jeans. Standing up straighter, he unfolds the paper and tosses it on the kitchen counter beside us before turning and retracing his steps to the couch and retrieving his shirt.

"What's that?"

"An offer to re-enlist and join my old spec ops team."

"You're going back to the military? Were you going to tell me?"

He shrugs with his back still facing me. "I just did."

"That's bullshit, Jay." I wipe away the last of the tears from my face. "Guess we're not so different after all, you and I."

His hand pauses on the doorknob as he glances over his shoulder at me. "We are different, Kat. Because I would've chosen you over the military. I would've always chosen you."

I move to take a step closer to him but he shakes his head. "Don't."

"Don't leave," I plead when he starts twisting the door handle.

"I'm in love with you, Katherine. And I'll always be there for you but right now I can't stand here and pretend that I don't."

I'm shaking my head when he looks over his shoulder at me. "I mean don't leave. Don't re-enlist."

As if on cue my phone rings. The slam of my front door echoes throughout my apartment behind him.

I wish I had told Jay the truth from the beginning, but I guess making something up and sticking with the lie was easier than having to admit the truth. That I was pregnant with his baby. And that I wanted to keep it. My entire life, I was convinced that I never wanted children because I never wanted to subject them to the same upbringing I had. I was afraid that I would end up exactly like my mother. It was my worst nightmare.

But now that I'm pregnant, I don't think I've been happier. Just knowing that there's a little person growing inside of me at this very moment warms my heart and brings a smile to my face.

I've been learning a lot about who I am and the type of person I want to be. And just when I thought life couldn't throw any more punches at me it proved me wrong when my phone rang with an unknown number.

"Hello?"

"Hello, is this Miss Katherine Young?" the older male voice asks.

"It is."

"My name's Arthur Williams. I'm sorry to inform you but your father, Chad Young, passed away last night."

"I'm sorry, what?"

I'm having a hard time processing what this man is telling me. My dad passed away last night. He was fine when I saw him last. I shut my eyes. It was months ago. The last time I saw my dad was months ago, and then ten years before that.

"Your father left me something to send to you in case of his death. Is your address still the same? Applewood Street?"

"Y-yes that's the right one."

"I will mail out the letter this afternoon then. I am sorry for your loss, Miss Young," he says then hangs up.

I don't even know where to go from here. My first instinct is to call Jason but as my thumb hovers over his name in my contact list I know that is no longer an option. I know he said that I didn't have to make up an excuse to call him or want to see him but the way he left earlier makes me believe that he no longer thinks that.

I scroll a few names up and text Alice instead.

"So, let me get this straight," Alice says making herself more comfortable on the barstool by my kitchen counter as I make us dinner, "you and Jay ended up in bed together months ago, after one too many tequila shots at the club. And you thought it was just a one-night stand but he told you he wanted more. Then you started working at Walker Advertising and met David. How am I doing so far?" Alice processes out loud.

"Pretty good but Jay never said anything about wanting to be together."

"Okay, so you go back to Toronto to see how your mom's doing after her stroke and when you get back to your hotel room Jay is there. You guys stay up all night talking and then have a romantic day exploring the city the next day."

"Correct."

"So then when you guys get back to town, you put the brakes on it again."

I shake my head. "No, that was after running into him at the pub and him telling me how I only want him when I'm drunk. But that didn't last long because I practically jumped him when he came over four days later."

"Then the next morning, you tell Jay it was a mistake to sleep with him?" Alice continues.

I cringe but confirm everything she's said so far.

"And you found out you're pregnant the day after you left the club together?"

"I never told him about the baby," I add.

"Why not?"

"Alice," I sigh, pinching the bridge of my nose between my thumb and forefinger, "even if I wanted to, what if Jay doesn't want this baby?"

"No, I get it," Alice defends. "But don't underestimate Jay. He'll be overjoyed knowing that you're carrying his child."

"I know," I sigh, linking my arms around her waist. "My thoughts and emotions are all over the place since finding out I'm pregnant and then finding out my dad passed away less than a week later. What if I just made the biggest mistake of my life and lost him?"

Alice pulls away but places her hands on my shoulders. "You didn't lose Jay. He'll come around."

I shake my head. "No, he won't. He got an offer to rejoin his old spec ops team. He's re-enlisting in the military."

"What? No, he's not."

"Yeah, he is, Alice. I saw the letter with my own two eyes."

Alice leans a hip against the counter and folds her arms across her chest narrowing her eyes at me. "You have to tell him, Kat. Before he gets on that plane."

"That sounds a little cliché."

"So? Who gives a fuck? You really want him getting on that plane and going to god-knows-where without knowing that he could be a dad?"

"Could be," I repeat back to her.

"When's your doctor's appointment?"

"Tomorrow."

"When does Jay fly out?"

I shrug my shoulders. "I have no idea."

She pulls her phone out from the back pocket of her jeans and her thumbs start flying over the screen.

"What are you doing?" I ask trying to see her screen.

"Texting Mike. He'll know when Jay flies out."

Less than a minute later her phone pings with a text.

"What did he say?" I'm so nervous I'm chewing on the cuticle on my thumb.

"He flies out in three days," she reads before looking up at me. "Your appointment is tomorrow. Once you find out for sure then you can tell him."

"What if he doesn't want anything to do with me?"

"Kat, stop. The guy has been madly in love with you for a while now."

I shake my head. "Alice, I can't be the reason he doesn't go back to doing something he wants to do."

"Katherine Marie Young, if that blood test comes back positive and you don't tell him, I will." Alice says, sticking her finger in my direction.

"Fine," I huff, feeling defeated. "You suck."

Alice grins and wiggles her eyebrows. "I do."

"Oh Jesus, I didn't need to know that." I roll my eyes and paste on my best disgusted face but it doesn't work and Alice and I are doubling over with laughter. We spend the rest of our night watching Disney movies and eating the butter chicken I made for us for dinner.

Before she leaves she hugs me again. "You know you're not alone in this. Whatever the results, Dani and I will be here for you."

"I know. Thank you, Alice."

"See ya later, Kat and George."

"George?"

Alice grins and quirks an eyebrow at my still flat stomach.

Oh hell no, she did not just name my non-existent baby bump.

After pouring myself the biggest glass of orange juice I could, I swipe the white envelope from the dining room table where it's been sitting for the last three days, and sit on my couch, pulling my legs up under me while grabbing the blanket off the back. With a deep inhale, I slip my finger under the tab and rip open the envelope, pulling out several pages decorated with my father's handwriting.

My dearest daughter,

If you are reading this that means my lawyer has contacted you. That also means that the cancer has finally won. The doctors say it's liver cancer and they're not sure how much longer I may have. I've refused any treatment they offered and I think I'll be okay to finally be at peace.

But before I go, I need to try and give you the answers to the questions I know you must have about your childhood. I don't think there is anything I could say that would make up for the years that I failed you as a father, and an apology just doesn't seem fitting after ten years but I must try.

Katherine, I am so sorry for not protecting you like a father should. I was weak and a coward, and I saw it in your eyes every time you would look at me.

My marriage to your mother was never easy. We found out she was pregnant when we were just sixteen and I thought I was doing the right thing by asking her to be my wife. After that our relationship was always strained.

Then you came along.

You were so perfect and every time you looked up at me with your big amber eyes, you smiled. Even then your mother refused to have anything to do with you and when she did hold you, you would cry until I picked you up. I should've known then that it would not be a good environment for you but I thought that the best place for you was with both your parents. Oh, how wrong I was.

The beatings didn't start until you were two and accidentally got into her makeup. My heart broke when I came home from work and saw the bruises marring your tiny body. And all for something so materialistic. But that was your mother, though; things were always more valuable to her than people.

You may not know this but I did threaten to leave her and take you with me. But Katherine, you must understand that even back then, fathers didn't have the same parental rights as the mothers did. Your mother threatened to call the police and charge with me kidnapping if I ever took you away. So, I stayed, but I couldn't stand the way she treated you or the scared look in your eyes every day. I turned to alcohol after that to numb the pain of seeing that fear in your eyes. I was in a constant state of drunkenness.

I know that none of this makes any of it easier to understand. You were my little girl and I knew if I left you behind with her she would never let me see you again and if I took you with me I would've ended up behind bars. It was a no-win situation.

I was also a coward. I should've stood up to her, demanded a divorce and pleaded with the courts for full custody of you given her treatments towards you but I never did.

I know saying sorry isn't going to cut it after all these years but I am sorry, Katherine. I wish I could've been the father you wanted. The father you *deserved.*

But you never needed me to, Katherine. You turned out to be a strong, passionate, successful woman. You are beautiful not just on the outside but on the inside. And I am proud to call you my daughter. I just hope and pray that you can heal from the past. I pray that you are able to love yourself and to realize that your past doesn't predict your future. I hope you know that you don't need another person's love to feel your worth.

You are worthy of love, Katherine. I should've told you that years ago, but I'm telling you now. Love yourself first. When you do that, everything will fall into place.

Also, I don't want you to come to the funeral. I don't say that out of malice. I say it out of a father's love for his daughter. For years, your mother had such a strong hold over you. Don't give that back to her again. You don't owe her anything. I never held you leaving against you. In fact, the day you left I couldn't have been more proud and relieved. Leave us behind in your past, Katherine.

If I only did one thing right in this world, it was having you as a daughter. I hope that one day you'll be able to forgive me.

Love,

Your father, Chad Young.

Tears stream down my face and my throat burns as I reread my father's last words. I cry for that little girl who was afraid of her mother and just wanted her father to love her. I cry for all those years that my father and I could've spent rebuilding our relationship if only we had reached out to each other and I wasn't so hell bent on punishing him.

He's right though, the apology is too little too late but I finally get it. I wasn't the only one living in fear of my mother. I was too young to see it then but I understand more about my father now. My hand flies to my still flat belly.

"It's just you and me now, George."

Yeah, I'm not naming my kid George.

~Twenty-two years ago~

When I wake up, it's like waking up in a dream. There are bright lights and a person in a white coat is standing over me.

"Am I dead?" I ask.

He laughs and shakes his head. My gaze slowly scans the room. There are tubes hooking me up to different machines, and my favorite pink blanket is sitting at the end of my bed. Someone must have brought it from my house when I was asleep. That is the only color visible in the stark white room; there are no flowers, no get well cards.

It is all evidence that no one cares about what happened. Then it hits me, where is my mother?

As if sensing what I am thinking, the doctor smiles gently.

"Your mother's on her way to see you. You should be able to leave in a couple days."

It was at that news that I turn and stare at him standing beside my hospital bed. Why would they send me back with her? It just didn't make any sense but they couldn't have known what she had done. Did they?

"You're lucky your dad found you when he did," he informs me as he places my chart back in the holder and smiles down at me.

"My dad?"

"He brought you in, said you'd fallen down the stairs at home. He found you when he got home from work."

"Is he still here?" I ask wishfully but already know the answer.

"He couldn't stay but he said he would be back tomorrow."

Tears start clouding my vision as what I just learned sinks in. My dad brought me to the hospital. He came home. But why didn't he tell them the truth about what happened? Why would he let them give me to her? Why was he being so cruel?

I don't want to go back. I wish that I could stay in this hospital room forever. Safe from my mother.

I like the nurses here, they all wear genuine smiles and were happy with my progress. They ask about school and what grade I am in and they ask what I like to do for fun. Every day is like a party in the pediatric ward. One of the nurses makes all the kids balloon animals and we get to hang them up from the ceiling in our rooms. Mine is a pink dog I named Pinky.

"Hi! Honey."

I turn my head at the familiar voice. She looks like an angel. Her brown hair cascading in loose curls framing her defined features. Her brown eyes sparkle with concern. To the outside world she looks like a concerned mother, worried about her only child.

I, however, know better. I know what she is capable of and I don't want to go home with her. Inside I plead with the doctor not to let her take me but what good will that do. They can't hear my thoughts and if they could they wouldn't understand.

Nobody understands.

"Hi, Momma" I reply

"How are you feeling?"

"Fine" I lie.

She seems happy with that answer as she takes a seat on the chair that is located on the left side of my bed.

"That was some show you put on for the doctors and all the nurses," she says, leaning in so that I am the only one who can hear her. "You know there are consequences for showing off and taking advantage of all these nice people," she snarls.

"I'm s-sorry," I reply, feeling the fear of her words creeping up my spine. I know what she means by consequences. That word usually means I will end up with another broken rib and quite possibly another broken nose and definitely some bruises to finish it off. It means wearing clothes that cover my body from the tops of my shoulders to the tips of my toes. It means pretending to be sick so that I won't have to participate in gym class.

I sigh, trying not to make it obvious. The scene that will enviably play out once I get home runs through my mind a dozen times. My eyes suddenly feel heavy and I am being dragged back into the darkness.

13 Anything For Her

Jason

"Eric has agreed to meet us at the warehouse late tonight," Cole informs us while we stand around the barbeque in Parker's backyard.

I nod in acknowledgement.

"Man, I can't believe you're re-enlisting," Parker slaps me on the shoulder handing me one of the beers between the fingers of his other hand.

"Never thought you would go back," Mike comments while flipping the burgers on the barbeque. It's November and about minus three degrees outside but in true Canadian fashion, we decided to fire up the barbeque instead of going out.

"Never thought I would be either," I reply, bringing the beer bottle up to my lips.

"Especially after the whole Kat thing," Mike mumbles, closing the lid on the barbeque.

That has me pausing. "What Kat thing?"

"You know, the whole pregnancy thing."

Parker punches Mike on the arm and I sputter and choke on the beer I just drank.

"What the fuck was that for?" Mike looks at Parker.

"Way to go, Jackass. He didn't know."

Mike's face falls when he finally turns to me and sees the shock that is clear across my face.

"Oh, shit man. I'm sorry."

The fuck just happened. Kat's pregnant.

"She's pregnant?" I ask, putting voice to my thoughts.

Parker and Mike don't say anything; they just stand there awkwardly holding their beers. A knowing look passes between them, then they're trying to look anywhere but directly at me.

"What? What am I missing?" I'm tired of all this beating around the bush bullshit. One of them is going to tell me what I want to know.

Mike shifts his weight from one foot to the other and runs his hand through his hair before finally meeting my eyes. "We overheard the girls talking earlier. It's yours."

Mine? "What- "

It doesn't take long for the memory of worshiping every inch of her skin to invade my head followed quickly by her telling me that what happened that night was a mistake.

Warmth spreads through my body at the thought of her possibly being pregnant with my child. If she is pregnant with my child, I will be the happiest fucking person on the planet. I still want more with her.

Fuck, I'd always want more with her.

My fists clench again with the realization that both Parker and Mike knew before I did. She could be pregnant with my child but it seems like I am the last one to know. That doesn't sit well with me. She should've fucking told me, even if it turns out not to be my kid.

Her muted laugh breaks through the screen door and my head snaps in her general direction. I knew she would be here. Parker and Danielle wanted to throw me a good-bye party before I left for god knows how long.

When my feet turn in her direction, I don't think twice about sliding open that screen door and walking up to her in the kitchen where she's sitting and talking with Danielle and Alice.

When she sees, me coming a small smile appears on her face. "Hi, Jay."

"We need to talk," I incline my head down the hallway grabbing her hand and pulling her behind me down the hall and into the guest bedroom.

"What did you want to talk about?" She asks innocently when I drop her hand and walk half way to the other side of the room.

"You're pregnant?" I turn to face her.

I can see the shock and uncertainty plain in her eyes and for a split-second I think she's going to lie to me and deny it but she just drops her chin to her chest and nods.

"Is it mine?"

She bobs her head refusing to look at me. "There was no one else." Her voice is so small that I have to strain to hear her.

"Why didn't you tell me, Kat?"

Her head snaps up at the anger underlining my voice. "And say what, Jay? That I didn't want to tell you and hold you back from rejoining your old team only to have you resent me for it later. Oh, and um, maybe because the last time I saw you it felt like you were walking away for good."

"Shit, you still believe that I won't come running every time you call. Fuck, Kat. I could never walk away from you for good. Don't you get that by now?"

"Everything okay in here?" Danielle asks, poking her head in the room.

When Kat turns to her with a warm smile, Danielle gives me a warning look before she closes the door behind her.

What the fuck was that look for?

I walk right up to Kat and place my fingers under her chin, gently turning her head to me again.

"Baby, I could never resent you. I would gladly drop everything for you. I've already told you that I would choose you over everything. Why can't you believe that?"

"Because it can't be reality," she whispers.

"Why?"

She curls her fingers around my arm holding her chin. "What you're offering, Jay. It only happens in the movies. I've spent my whole life only seeing the worst in people. In myself. It's hard not to when you've had it beaten into you, literally. So when someone like you says that they would always choose me, I can't believe it cause it's not possible." She pushes on my arm and steps back causing my hand to fall away.

"Kat –" I go to reach for her again but she shakes her head and holds a hand up to stop me.

"I love you Jason. It took me a while to realize it, but I do. I

123

love you. And not in the platonic sense of the word either. Somewhere along the line I fell in love with my best friend."

"Kat, I- "

"Let me finish. Please," she begs with tears swimming behind her eyes.

I bite my tongue and motion for her to continue.

"I'm in love with you, Jason. But I can't give you all of me right now. I'm so broken and you deserve someone who is whole. It's not fair to you to keep you on the back burner waiting for the day when I'm finally ready for you to love me back. I'm not going to ask you to stay, but I'm not going to tell you to go either because I'm fucking selfish."

"You can be as much a part of our child's life as you want. But I can't be with you. I can't give that piece of myself to you and I don't know if I'll ever be ready to. I'm going to take my father's advice and try to love myself first."

Well, the baby will be first, but I get what she's saying.

I shake my head. "Kat."

I want to tell her that I don't care if she's broken. I fell in love with her when she was broken and I'd gladly help her put the pieces of herself back together. I'd happily volunteer to show her how amazing she is and why I fell in love with her. But she doesn't give me the opportunity when she slowly walks up to me. Placing her hands on my shoulders and standing on her tiptoes she places a soft kiss on my cheek. And then she's the one who turns away and walks out the door.

I feel like our relationship has done a one-eighty. Before it was always me turning away and walking out the door of her apartment. I was the one who left her standing on the other side of the door. But now I am the one who is left standing, forced to watch as the other piece of me just walks away.

I understand where she is coming from. I understand her need to try and finally heal from the damage of her childhood and to love herself first. But learning to love herself first doesn't mean she has to give up those who love her too.

And I'm not David. I am not about to make her a pawn in some game. She may not want me to stick around but I am going to fight for her. I am not giving up on the idea of us. I don't care if it takes her five months or five years to be ready to give us a chance. I'm not going anywhere.

Running my hand through my hair.

I really need to get a haircut.

I scroll down to the number I'm looking for and hit dial. He isn't going to like what I am about to do but he would understand that I have to do it.

"Smith," his voice booms from the other end.

"It's Jay."

"Jason," Mae greets me with a warm smile as she motions for me to come in.

"Hi, Mae," I lean in, placing a kiss on her cheek.

A blush creeps up her face as she tries to smack me with the dish towel in her hands. "He's in his office." She tips her head down the hall.

Tipping my chin in a silent thank you, I make my way towards his office door as she goes back to the kitchen. The smells coming from that side of the house are making my mouth water and I'm slightly regretting that I won't be staying for dinner after what I'm about to do.

"Come in," Smith's voice sounds from the other side of the door when I knock. "Jason," he greets, standing up and holding out his hand for me to shake after I close the door behind me.

"Sir."

After we shake hands, he eyes me for a second from behind eyes that look eerily similar to my emerald ones. There were countless times when I used to wish that this man was my father. He was often more of a father to me than my own. It wasn't that I had a bad childhood; my dad was just never home long enough to have anything more than a business relationship with me. He was always working to provide for us.

"You're not accepting my offer," he guesses correctly.

My shoulders slump. "Look, Tyler. I appreciate the offer, and under any other circumstance I would've jumped at it…"

"She's a lucky woman," he interrupts me, a knowing look adorning his face.

"Sir?"

He chuckles. "Boy, I might be getting old but I'm certainly not going blind. I saw the way she looked at you when you brought her for dinner. And the way you looked at her."

There's a faraway look in his eyes and a small smile on his face as he slowly shakes his head. "I can't say I blame you for not wanting to re-enlist. Mae's about ready to have me home for good now too."

"She's pregnant," I blurt out.

His lips lift in a smile as he stands to congratulate me and shake my hand again. But that smile fades when we sit back down and he sees my brows furrow.

"Whatever you're thinking right now, Miller, stop."

I let my eyes lazily draw up to meet his. The man sitting before me is no longer a friend but my CO. He levels a finger at me, staring me down. "The only thing your father did wrong was work too hard to make sure you and your mom were provided for."

"I don't want to follow in his footsteps, Tyler. I don't want to wake up one day and realize that it's too late to get to know my kid because they hate me for never being around. And Kat…I can tell she's afraid that she'll end up just like her mother."

"Jason, from what I saw that night at dinner, that woman could never harm a fly. Unless it threatens someone she loves. I can't see her being anything like her mother. If anything, that kid will be spoiled with the two of you as parents," he grins.

"Thank you, Sir." I push my way out of my chair and towards his office door. Before I can turn the handle something nags at me. "You seem awfully calm for just being told that your only recommendation for your position is no longer an option," I say, turning back to him.

Smith grins, leaning back in his chair. "I told you, Miller. I may be getting old but I'm not going blind. The minute I saw you with that girl I knew there was no way you were going to accept my offer. Your phone call and visit today just confirmed what I already knew. Drake will be taking over for me when I retire. You'll always have a position on the team though, Miller."

I laugh. "You were always one step ahead of us."

I hear him chuckle behind me as I close his office door and make my way back to my car.

"You're just not going to tell her that you didn't get on the plane this morning?" Mike asks as we're walking into the gym.

"Nope," I respond, pulling open the glass door.

"What *are* your plans?" Parker asks, sitting down on the bench, switching his outdoor shoes for his gym ones.

"Porter hasn't filled my spot on the team yet so I can come back."

"And what about Kat?"

"I'm going to give her the time she needs but I plan on sending her money to help out with the baby."

"So, what? You're going to avoid her so she thinks you left?" Mike asks as we head to the locker room.

"No. I'm just not going to tell her that I didn't leave.

The next time I see her will be on her terms. When she's ready." I step onto the treadmill and before I start my usual ten-kilometer warm up, I level a stare at Mike. "And don't go telling her either. I'm serious, Mike. Next time she and I come face to face again it will be on her terms."

Mike holds up his hands palms up before starting his own warm up run. "I won't say anything."

"Yeah, right," Parker laughs from my other side.

"What?" Mike looks over at him.

"You sing like a canary whenever Alice smiles up at you."

"Fuck you. Like you don't do the same thing with Danielle."

"All right, ladies, can we just get back to our regularly-scheduled work out?" I interrupt, increasing the speed on my treadmill.

14. ONE CALL AWAY

Katherine

"Ola!" Alice sings, pushing past the door of my apartment with Danielle on her heels.

"Alice," I sigh, "you're not Spanish."

"Jesus, who died in here?" Danielle comments, taking in the current state of my apartment.

"What are you guys doing here?" I ask, grabbing the stack of plates from my coffee table and walking them over to the sink.

"Well, at least she's been eating." Danielle looks at Alice with a raised eyebrow.

Alice agrees, removing a t-shirt from the arm of the couch by her fingertips and looking at it in utter disgust, like she's afraid it might suddenly give her cooties. "Seriously, this is worse than the state of Danielle's condo during her drunken binge."

"Hey!" Danielle exclaims, folding her arms across her chest.

"What are you guys doing here?" I repeat.

Danielle uncrosses her arms and moves towards me. "We're pulling best friend duty."

"Yup, so march that perky ass of yours to the shower while we attempt to dig your apartment out from under this mess."

"Look, guys, I appreciate what you're trying to do but I don't feel like going anywhere today and neither do I feel like sharing, so you're wasting your time."

"That's good because we didn't plan on going anywhere. We're staying in, ordering pizza, and watching sexy Derek Morgan chase down bad guys," Alice grins.

"And you're not going to ask about Jay?" I ask, raising an eyebrow skeptically at my two best girlfriends.

"Not unless you start the conversation," Danielle reassures me.

"Fine, you win. I'll go shower."

"Thank fuck," Alice mutters right before I close the bathroom door.

As the warm water runs down my body, I'm helpless to prevent the memories of Jay in my apartment from invading. A close up of his smiling emeralds and cocky smirk appear before my closed eyes. I sigh remembering the way his hands felt on my body. Remembering the way feeling his warm breath on my skin would cause goose bumps to appear, and the way he would follow them with his tongue from my collarbone all the way down to my stomach before placing open-mouthed kisses on my hips. The way he would worship all my curves, placing kisses on all the places of my body I was embarrassed about or didn't like.

The feel of my hand skimming down my stomach rouses me from the trance created by the onslaught of memories and reality crashes in. And the reality is, I'm being a coward and I regret telling him that night was a mistake. Reality also includes finding out Jay re-enlisted in the military, learning that my father passed away only to receive a letter the following week that he wrote when he found out he was dying, and getting answers to some of my questions about my childhood but knowing it was too late. And finally, I'm crushed by the memory of the look on Jay's face when I walked away from him at Danielle and Parker's place.

I lean the back of my head against the wet tile, tears roll down my face as everything in my mind goes silent except for one word.

Jason.

I have been such a fucking coward. I thought I could be happy without him, that maybe he wasn't my future because I was too fucking scared to admit the truth. The truth is, I have always been in love with my best friend. Our friendship happened fast. From the minute we met at Gotcha's when Danielle, Alice and I first moved to Oceanview, our friendship was almost instantaneous. It started as after work drinks and hanging out when the six of us would get together for barbeques, pub nights, or for one of Bella's hockey games, and it morphed into weekend hikes and camping trips, road trips that lead nowhere, late night phone calls and random text messages. Soon we were constantly texting or calling each other, and if we weren't then we were together.

I don't know when it happened but like I told him, somewhere along the line I fell in love with my best friend and that scared the ever-living shit out of me. I didn't know how to love someone and I sure as heck didn't know how to accept someone's love. When I finally got up the courage to tell him, I didn't even give him a chance to respond. I just tucked my tail between my legs and ran like a bat out of hell.

And now…well now he was god knows where for god knows how long. I missed my chance at something real because of fear.

The stupid bitch.

Jay never stopped believing in us for one minute. Even when I drove him crazy. Even when I called him a mistake.

He never gave up.

But he did finally give up though, didn't he? Because if he hadn't given up he would have never re-enlisted. He would've shown up at my door sometime during this past week. He would still be here fighting for us. But he wasn't. And I didn't know if he ever would be again.

"Well, shit. I didn't think it was possible, but you look worse than when we sent you in there," Alice comments when I finally make my way back out into the living room.

"Ha-ha, very funny. Please tell me pizza is on its way," I prod, slumping back down on the couch and throwing the heated blanket over my yoga pants clad legs.

I hate to admit it, but the two of them did a bang-up job of cleaning my apartment. I would've gotten to it…eventually. It was just that I had zero energy this past week. This pregnancy has been kicking my ass and add regret over letting him go on top of that and it wasn't a priority on my list of things to do, which is not like me. I become a clean freak when I have too much on my mind and need to work through some things, but not this time. Cleaning just reminded me of the last time I went nuts on a cleaning spree. It was the same night Jay and I had slept together again.

Yes, I know that's a lame excuse but I'm sticking with it.

"One pineapple and one pepperoni are on their way," Danielle says, sticking her feet under the opposite side of the blanket.

"Good, I'm starving," I reply, reaching for the remote and turning on the TV.

"Eating for two already?" Alice quips handing Danielle and I each a virgin strawberry daquiri.

Alice and Danielle laugh when I level Alice with my best death glare and give her the finger.

"What's going on in that head of yours, Kat?" Dani asks, taking a sip of her drink.

"I miss Jay," I sigh, leaning further into the back of the couch and propping my feet up on the coffee table.

Danielle grins and squeezes my hand. "You never heard this from us, but he never re-enlisted."

"What do you mean he never re-enlisted?"

"He never got on that plane, Kat. He's been in town this whole time."

"Why didn't he tell me?"

I sound like a broken record.

"Because you told him you needed some time alone." Alice settles back in the recliner. "He was just respecting your wishes. He figured that when you were ready you would find a way to reach out to him."

My hands fly to my temples and I dig my fingers into them, massaging tiny circles while shutting my eyes. I feel like my head is spinning with all this new information.

He put his career on the line for me and never asked for anything in return. And then finding out that he never re-joined his old team because of me. It is too much. I feel the pressure building up inside of me, about to explode.

Then it detonates.

What am I still doing sitting here? The man I love risked not only his career in the police department but also gave up re-enlisting in the military for me. He fought to defend me against someone who didn't think twice about ruining my life. He was not only willing to put my happiness before his but he was willing to put his life on hold for me. I was a fucking idiot living with blinders on.

Until now.

He pays attention to me, he knows when something is bothering me and if I want to talk about or not. He knows just what to say to make me want to talk. He listens to me and doesn't complain when I go off on one of my rants about dolphins, or orcas, or animal captivity. He doesn't think I'm crazy for believing that they deserve as much respect as any human does. He doesn't think that my passion is stupid.

He gets it. He gets me.

Suddenly, I don't care that it is raining like crazy outside. I need to find him and apologize and grovel and hope to god that he still loves me enough to forgive me and give us a chance.

The minute I jump up from the couch in my realization and resolve to find him, I know something isn't right. As soon as I stand up straight, I almost immediately double-over in pain. The cramps are sudden and unbearable. And there is blood, I see so much blood when I glance down right before the room spins and goes black. The last thing I hear are Dani and Alice yelling my name before my body is in a free fall.

15. Sometimes I Pray
Jason

The back tires of my truck slide as I turn the corner onto the street the hospital is located on. The Toyota Tundra corrects itself almost within inches of hitting the oncoming Mazda. I know I'm going too fast for the freezing rain that's currently falling, but I couldn't give a damn right now.

As soon as I got the call from Parker, I was in the truck and racing down the highway. It didn't hurt that I had the siren going; the other drivers probably just figured I was in one of the RCMP's undercover vehicles and gave me the right of way.

Tires squealing, I pull into the emergency parking lot, throw the truck in park and jump out. *I'll figure out parking later.* They could tow it for all I care. My only concern right now is getting to Kat.

Mike pushes through the emergency room entrance, making his way towards me. "Parker's in the waiting room. I'll take care of your parking pass." He pats my shoulder reassuringly before I take off running down the long hallway.

I have no idea what happened to her. All I know is that Dani called Parker in tears telling him he needed to find me because something had happened to Kat. But the scene that greets me when I turn the corner into the waiting room has my heart stopping. Parker is consoling a crying Danielle. And Alice, the girl who never cries and who doesn't let anything get to her, has mascara streaked tears running down her cheeks.

Oh god.

"Where is she?" My breathing sounds labored and I don't know if it's due to running through the hospital like a madman or because I had to consciously remind myself to breathe.

Parker slowly disentangles himself from Danielle and stands to greet me. "Dr. Reynolds is with her now."

"What happened?"

New sobs sound from behind him.

"Jay, you might want to sit down, man."

"Just tell me, Parker. What happened to Kat?"

"He's right, Jay. You need to sit down for this," Mike adds, walking in behind me.

"Fine." I sit in the first open seat next to Danielle. "Now, can someone please tell me what the hell is going on with my girl?"

Parker runs a hand through his hair and Mike nervously tucks his hands into the pockets of his jeans. *What the hell?* Their actions are starting to piss me off. I haven't allowed myself to think the worst and overreact until I knew for sure what had happened. But seeing the way these two are acting has me wanting to search every inch of this hospital until I find her.

"Jay," Parker rubs the back of his neck before dropping his hand and meeting my eyes, "they said it looks like she may have had a miscarriage."

He was right, I did need to be sitting because if I were standing right now, my knees would've given out. As it is, I have a hard time breathing, or processing what he just said.

My baby. Our baby.

My head drops to between my legs and I'm struggling to take deep breaths as the weight of what he just said crashes in on me.

Kat lost our baby.

A pair of black leather dress shoes appear in my field of vision and when I follow them up, Dr. Reynolds is looking directly at me, concern lacing his eyes. Parker, Mike, and I grew up knowing him as part of our families. Sam Reynolds grew up with and went to school with our fathers. So, even though we aren't related by blood, the three of us still consider him family. He and his wife never had kids but the three of us kept the Reynolds on their toes just as much as we did our own parents.

"Jason." He pats my knee lowering himself down into the chair next to mine.

"How is she?"

"Physically, she'll be okay. Mentally, it's going to take a while for her to heal from this. You need to be there for her, Jason, now more than ever. Even when she retreats into herself."

I crane my head up to look at him. "I always was, doc."

A small smile appears on his face. "You've been in love with her for a long time."

I shake my head sitting back up in my seat and running my palms down my thighs. "A year is hardly that long."

A small chuckle sounds from his throat, "You fell in love with her the minute you met her that night a couple years ago. Donna and I could see it in your face when you came for dinner the next day. Tyler and Mae knew it too." Sam pushes his hands into his knees as he stands up again. It didn't surprise me that these people knew I was in love before I did.

"Don't give up on her, Jason. She's still sleeping but you can go see her now. Room 3A." Just as quickly as he appeared, he disappears around the corner and heads off to another patient.

"Let's go," Parker claps me on the back and inclines his head in the direction of Kat's room.

She looks so peaceful in her sleep but I know that can't be further from the truth. I can't imagine what she's going through now or what she'll have to experience from here on out. I can't begin to put myself in her shoes right now, to know that you were pregnant and about to be a mom in one minute to having that taken from you in the next.

I gently slip my hand under hers so as not to wake her and not disrupt the IV. Sam's right. She's going to need me now more than ever. Even when she denies it and withdraws into herself. If there was ever a time that I had to show just how much I love this woman and just how much I would fight for her and stand by her, now was that time.

I didn't care if after this, she decided that she still didn't want to be with me. As long as I knew that she was healthy and safe and happy, then I could walk away.

I *would* walk away if it means her happiness.

Smith said my position on the team was always open whenever I decided to re-enlist. If I had to walk away from Kat, I don't think

I could stand by and watch her with anyone else; it would hurt to see the woman I love fall in love with another man. At that point, I will board the plane without looking back.

"You need to eat something, Kat." Alice's voice carries through the door.

"Seriously, fuck off, Alice. I'm not eating that shit," Kat screeches.

That's my girl.

Kat has been home from the hospital almost a week now, but she's confined herself to her bedroom or the couch where she watches reruns of *Gilmore Girls* on Netflix all day long. And when she's not watching Netflix, she's sleeping.

I think I'll take hours of TV show reruns over her sleeping all day. When I first brought her home, she slept for two days straight. She barely ate anything and it was a chore to get her to at least drink water to keep herself hydrated. On the third day, Alice and Danielle came over and convinced her to get out of bed and move to the couch. So, she did. She's been alternating between bed and the couch ever since.

"I brought cheeseburgers," I call over my shoulder, making my way into the kitchen.

"Oh, thank goodness," Kat groans from the couch.

"You can't keep eating that junk food shit," Alice says to her before turning to me, "and you have to stop enabling her."

I shrug and paste a sheepish grin on my face. "I'm a grown man who works out five days a week. I need the protein."

"I would literally kill for a greasy cheeseburger right now." Kat throws her blanket off and holds out her hands for me to toss her one. She catches it effortlessly.

Alice wrinkles her nose in disgust when Kat unwraps the

burger. "That's so gross. I can smell the grease from here." She grabs her purse from the floor and tugs on her jacket while she walks to the door. "You guys enjoy your fast food."

"Oh, we will!" I take a huge bite out of my burger and, with my mouth full, shoot Alice a closed mouth smile.

She rolls her eyes. "So gross."

Kat is giggling on the couch when Alice closes the door behind her. The sound is music to my ears. It's the first time she's laughed in over a week.

"What'd she bring you anyway?" I ask after I've chewed and swallowed.

"Veggie stir-fry."

"And?"

She shakes her head, "And nothing. That's it."

"That's it? No meat?"

"Nope."

"Well, then," I pick up the bag with the other two burgers from the counter and make my way over to her, "I think I saved the day."

She nods and then her eyes drift close when she takes the first bite. "Bacon," she says dreamily.

"I don't know whether to be jealous of that bacon making you sound like that or turned on," I tease.

"Shut up." She playfully back-hands my chest grinning.

"Just calling it like I see it." I hold my hands out laughing.

"Hey, want to go snowboarding this weekend? They're expecting fresh powder on the mountain this week," Kat says as we're gathering all the empty burger wrappers from our meal.

"You sure you're feeling up to it?"

She frowns, crossing her arms over her chest and leaning a hip into the kitchen counter. "I need to get out of here, Jay. Even if it's just for a day. I've been cooped up here along enough."

Soon after she woke up in the hospital, Dr. Reynolds had to deliver the heart-breaking news to her about the miscarriage. He said it was caused by insulin resistance due to her Polycystic Ovary Syndrome, or PCOS as he called it, which prevented the endometrial lining from maturing. *Whatever that means.* He tried explaining it again to me but it just sounded complicated.

"Then why don't we go to Harrison Hot Springs instead. Or we could drive up to Vernon and spend the weekend at Sparkling Hill."

She grins. "A weekend at the spa and wine tours in the Okanagan sounds like a plan."

I shake my head, a small half grin pulling at the corner of my mouth. "Only you would find a way to add wine into the mix."

"Damn straight." Her grin morphs into a full smile

"Then Sparkling Hill it is. I'll come by after work on Friday and pick you up."

16. Barrel of His Gun
Katherine

I'm excited to spend the weekend alone with Jay at a spa resort almost an hour outside of our city. This is going to be the first opportunity for us to be alone together since the hospital, and I am looking forward to it.

I am looking forward to it so much that I may have picked up a little something sexy to wear this weekend. I know that I was determined to keep him strictly in the friend-zone but despite all of my efforts, he still managed to break down all the barriers I put up.

Okay, so maybe my efforts were lacking a little in some areas. Or all areas.

Okay, maybe I wasn't trying all *that* hard to keep him in the friend-zone. But can you blame me? The guy is built like a freaking Greek god. Trust me, if you saw him you would understand why my efforts were lacking.

Just as I'm leaving the lingerie store, my phone rings. A smile tugs at my lips when I glance down to check the number.

"Miss me already?" I tease, answering on the second ring.

A deep male chuckle sounds from the other side and I have to hold back the moan that's threatening to escape as I make my way across the parking lot to my car. Just the sound of his voice is enough to get my body worked up.

"Mike wants to go to wing night tonight. You down? He says Alice will be there and Parker's calling Dani now."

"Wing night sounds good. I could do with a night out."

"That's what I thought."

I can hear the smile in his voice but before I have a chance to answer him, a strong arm wraps around my middle with a hand covering my mouth to quiet my screams and I'm being drawn back and up against a male body. I can hear Jay yelling my name from my cell phone laying on the ground next to my car where I dropped it, and then the distinct sound of crushing glass.

I'm trying to use any and all strength I can find to fight off my kidnapper while he tries to stuff me in what I suspect is the trunk of a car. That's when I get a good look at him and my body stills.

David.

An evil smirk plays across his mouth right before he shuts the trunk and my world goes dark. Memories of me trapped naked under him while he held a knife to my throat and started touching me invade my mind. My stomach rolls and it takes all of my concentration not to get sick in the trunk.

Jay will find me; it'll be okay.

"It'll be okay," I repeat back to myself as my body gets jolted from side to side by the bumps in the road.

17. DAVID

Despite the calendar saying December, it still hasn't snowed yet in Oceanview. Fall-colored leaves crunch beneath my feet as I hike further into the forest. I like coming out here in the early hours of the morning before the runners are out here getting in their daily workouts before work.

It's quiet.

Peaceful.

I inhale deeply the scents of nature, while birds sing from high tree branches as they wake up for the day. The city hasn't touched this part of paradise yet and right now, it's all mine.

Rustling next to my boot draws my attention down and I give it a good hard kick, making it stop. This is the other reason why I love it out here at this time of morning.

It's private.

Nobody for miles, and that allows me to dispose of my prey.

Runners and hikers stick to the outlined trails out here; nobody really goes off the beaten path and that is the perfect opportunity.

I crouch down and slowly unzip the duffle bag to my right. Amber eyes stare up at me in horror. Muffled screams and sobs escape her throat but not loud enough to alert anyone to my presence. Soft kissable lips wrap around a strip of cloth. Her tan skin is so smooth, like silk. She had been so much fun, but she and her RCMP friends have ruined my life.

Now she is going to pay with hers.

Her boyfriend and his friends thought they could threaten me. That the motorcycle club wouldn't have my back. They were wrong, but I was still tasked with getting rid of her to send a message to her boyfriend. No one fucks with the Knight's MC.

My finger comes up to my pursed lips. "Shh."

Grabbing a hold of her rope bound hands, I haul her up and over my shoulder in a fireman's hold. I am never more grateful that I had the good sense to bind her ankles too because as soon as I have her over my shoulder she tries to land a kick to my balls but I expertly dodge it.

She is a feisty one.

I walk the two feet to the hole I had dug earlier in the week and drop her down, her head bouncing off the cold ground and momentarily blacking her out. A smirk tugs at the corner of my mouth as I pull my 9mm from the back waistband of my tailored black suit pants, and aim it right between those pretty amber eyes.

A gunshot rings out causing the birds to flee their posts on the surrounding tree branches.

18. Hold On To Me
Jason

"Kat! Katherine!"

I hear several pairs of boots running behind me as I dodge tree branch after tree branch to try and get closer to where David's body now lays lifeless,

As soon as I figured out what happened when I heard Kat's scream and then the line go silent, I tracked down her cell signal and had the guys meet me at the store. When I found out that the store had surveillance cameras facing the parking lot due to a series of car break-ins, I was enormously thankful. Then when I saw David take her it was like I lost all control. It took me almost all night to track down his whereabouts.

I had warned him to stay away from her. Hell, I threatened the guy and did a pretty sizable number on his face and limbs. But I should've just killed him when I had the chance back at the warehouse. Would it have cost me my career in the RCMP and the military? Yeah, it fucking would have. But Kat would be safe. And right now, that's all I care about.

But moments ago, as I came up and saw him pointing that gun down I didn't bat an eye when I pulled the trigger. The son-of-a-bitch kidnapped my girl and was about to kill her. Saving her and making sure that he would never hurt her again was my number one priority.

As I get closer, muffled screams and sobs sound from the shallow grave right in front of where he was standing.

"Call an ambulance!" I yell over my shoulder, not caring who's behind me as her tied up body comes into view and I drop to my knees to untie her hands as Mike drops down as well to help me untie her ankles.

As soon as we get her untied, her fingers claw their way up my arms until she can wrap her arms around my neck while I help her out of the grave. She collapses in a heap in my arms while she buries her face in my neck and cries.

"Shh, it's over. I have you," I soothe, wrapping her tighter in my arms.

"Ambulance and coroner are on their way," Parker says, making his way back over to us from the trail.

At his voice, she looks up at me and over to him before her eyes roam over to David's body.

"Kat. I gently place my hand on her cheek and move her face over to me again. "You don't need to see that."

"You killed him." It isn't so much a question as it is a statement.

I nod slightly. "I did. I should've done it sooner," I add, dropping my head.

"Thank you," she whispers, linking her arms back around my neck and pressing her soft lips to mine.

"You don't need to thank me, Kat. As long as I'm alive I will always protect you." Taking her hand, I stand and help her up before wrapping an arm around her shoulders. "Come on. Let's get you checked out."

Once I get Kat settled back at my house and make sure she's okay. I head back out and meet up with the guys at the warehouse.

"Knight," I tip my chin in greeting at the newest member of the group.

"Miller. I heard what happened to Kat tonight. Shit man, I'm sorry." He grips my hand and we shake before moving back to our respective corners.

"We took care of it."

Eric nods. "David was getting to be a nuisance, but my dad's going to start asking questions when he doesn't turn up."

"Will that be an issue?" Parker inquires.

Eric eyes up Parker before shaking his head. "It shouldn't. I'll handle it."

"Are you sure you want to go through with this, Knight? Taking down your dad's MC could be dangerous for all of us," Parker reiterates what we've discussed previously.

"Fuck yeah, I'm sure. Those sick bastards need to go down. I haven't been able to do that on my own so when Cole approached me asking about more information on the club, I knew this was the way to do it."

"What branch of government are you?" Mark asks.

"You mean before they abandoned me? CSIS."

Curses sound all around. CSIS is the Canadian equivalent to the CIA. And if they were involved, then this case is bigger than we all originally thought.

"How's Kat doing?" Parker slaps a hand on my back.

"Not sure, man. She's had a fucked-up couple months. But Dani and Alice should be there with her now."

"Alice Johnson?" Eric questions.

I nod, narrowing my eyes at him and feel Parker and Mark straighten next to me. After all this shit with Kat, we'll all be more protective over those girls.

"Cole mentioned her name in passing. Alice and I grew up together."

Eric spends the next few minutes explaining to us how he was forced to leave and move in with his father when he was still in high school, and hadn't known that his father ran a motorcycle club. He also explains his reasoning for not contacting Alice in the last fourteen years.

Before going our separate ways until the next meeting, we all agree that it would be in her best interest if Eric kept a low profile while he was back in town and didn't make any contact with her.

19. IN LOVE WITH MY BEST FRIEND

Jason

Kat's face is a mixture of confusion and excitement when she steps out of her apartment building and sees me pulling up. I told her that our trip to Sparkling Hill could wait another week but being as stubborn as she is, she insisted that she was okay, and that she needed a weekend away now more than ever.

"How'd you convince Mike to let you borrow his beloved Audi R8?" she inquires as I run around to the passenger side of the car and take her bag from her and help her into the car.

"He owed me a favor," I grin settling back into the driver's seat.

"Do I even want to know what type of favor it was for him to let this car out of his sight for a weekend?"

I chuckle, slipping the car into gear. "Probably not."

She laughs, reaching over and turning up the country radio station as Old Dominion plays over the speakers. We drive in silence for the majority of the way enjoying the scenery and music.

Katherine

"Wow." My breath leaves me when we walk into our suite.

On the opposite side of the room is a floor-to-ceiling glass window that spans almost the entire length of the room. A two-person jetted tub sits in one corner overlooking breathtaking views of Lake Okanagan and an uninterrupted view of the Monashee Mountains. On the other side of the suite is a sitting area in front of an amazing gas fireplace. A door is positioned next to the fireplace, and I'm assuming it'll lead to the bedroom. My suspicions are confirmed when Jay disappears through the door with our bags and returns empty handed.

"Jay." My eyes roam over the remarkable suite again before finding his. "You didn't need to do this."

He crosses his arms over his chest and leans against the wall, crossing one foot over the other and studying me. "I know I didn't *need* to, but I wanted to. Think of it as an early Christmas present,

Kat." He uncrosses his arms and walks over to me. "You've been through a lot these past few months. You deserve this," he says, indicating to the room.

"Thank you," I reach up, placing a kiss on his cheek.

He tucks both his hands in the pockets of his jeans like he's afraid that if he doesn't restrain his hands somehow, he'll end up touching me. "So, what's first? Spa massage? Or dinner and wine?"

"Dinner sounds good. I'm starving." As if on cue, my stomach lets out the loudest growl I've ever heard.

"All right," he laughs. "Let's get some food in you before we wake the bear."

"Ha-ha, very funny. You're just a regular comedian aren't you," I tease as I put my jacket on again.

He ruffles my hair, chuckling at the dirty look I try to throw him before grabbing the key card to our room. "Come on, smartass. Let's go get dinner.

"I'm so stuffed," I groan, slumping back onto the couch once we get back to the suite.

"Agreed," he confirms, taking up a seat next to me and patting his belly. "I feel like I gained ten pounds." His head lazily rolls to face me. "But it was worth it for that bacon," he grins. "All right," he says as he pats my knee before rising from the couch. "I'm going to shower, and then how about I start a fire and we watch a movie?"

"Sounds good," I nod, excited for a relaxing night with him in front of the fire.

"What movie did you pick?" he asks, walking out of the bedroom looking sexy as all fuck, shirtless with a pair of jeans riding low on his hips.

"*Suicide Squad*," I beam up at him.

He groans as he drops down next to me on the couch. "Again? How many times do you plan on watching it?" he teases.

I grin over at him and in that moment, with the light from the fireplace and the moonlight streaming in from the window, I know that I've never seen another man as handsome as he is. And that no matter what, this man will always own my heart.

His eyes dart down to my lips when I drag my teeth along my bottom lip, then back up to my eyes. He's like a magnet and I'm powerless to his pull, and not entirely certain that I want to fight it anymore.

"Jason, I..." my voice, a little more than a whisper, cuts out. I don't know how to go about trying to explain to him how I am feeling. This past week, especially, has made realize just how precious and short life is. I am done pretending and lying to myself. I love him with all of my heart, and I am ready for him to love me back.

He cups the back of my neck in his hand and leans his forehead against mine. My eyes drift close and I will myself to just be in this moment with him, to just drink in the feeling of his skin on mine.

"I know." He pulls back and places a soft kiss on my forehead, removing his hand.

Those two little words make me curse myself for all the times I pushed him away. He thinks that I was about to tell him we had to stay friends, that I don't want this. I'm such an idiot.

Now that he's moved away and is no longer touching me, it's like my world has gone cold. I'm aching to feel his skin on mine again, to be in his arms again. That's exactly what I need; to get lost in his body and his touch. To let him carry my burdens for a little while.

I find myself moving closer to him on the couch in our suite, moving a lock of hair that has fallen on his forehead back, and tracing my fingers down his square jaw to his neck and eventually down to trace the top of the large tattoo that spans half his chest, up his shoulder and down to his elbow. His skin is still slightly wet from his shower.

"Kat…"

My eyes drift up to emerald ones that have gone a shade darker and then down to his lips. "I'm sorry. I'm so fucking sorry, Jay." I throw one of my legs over his and straddle him over his jeans while my mouth explores his jaw line, my teeth playfully nipping at his earlobe, before making my way back to his mouth when he groans. "Show me how much you love me."

His mouth has done wicked things to my body both in reality and in my dreams. I'm not ashamed to admit that my dirty dreams about Hugh Jackman were eventually replaced by dirty dreams of Jason Miller and his wicked mouth and hands.

Seriously, the guy is gifted, and could probably talk a nun out of her underwear.

His hands run up my thighs and grip my hips before slipping under my long sleeve shirt. His fingers gently skim over my skin while he drags my shirt up and over my head. His mouth comes down to place kisses down my neck to my collarbone and then down between my breasts while his hands slide up my back and grip my shoulders. My head tips slightly back giving him easier access.

He doesn't waste any more time, undoing my bra next and then his mouth is right back to placing kisses on the tops of my breast before his tongue circles my nipple, drawing it into his mouth. A moan escapes my throat when his teeth gently tug on it and then his tongue licks away the sting before repeating the action to the other one.

He takes his time worshipping my body with his hands and mouth, and I can feel him getting hard through his jeans. I rake my nails down each of his arms, not hard enough to leave a mark but hard enough that it makes his dick jump behind the denim fabric and elicits another groan from him. Jason's breath hitches when I slip my hand under his waistband, surprised to notice that he's not wearing any boxers, and wrap my fingers around his dick, stroking up and down. His eyes drift shut and his head falls back against the couch.

I stroke him a few more times before removing myself from his lap to stand up. His eyes open and his head snaps up when he realizes that my hand is no longer wrapped around his dick. His eyebrow raises when he sees the small playful smirk on my face.

Silently, I turn around and look over my shoulder as I hook my thumbs into the waistband of my leggings, bend at my hips a little and ever so slowly proceed to pull my leggings down and over my ass an inch at a time. I'm fully bent over by the time I have them pulled down, and hear him groan behind me.

When I stand up again and step out of them he's right behind me, moving my hair off my shoulder and placing open-mouthed kisses along my shoulder, up my neck, and on each of the bruises still left behind from David. Jason's hands grip my hips before spinning me around to face him. His mouth devours mine. Our mouths don't disconnect from each other while he thumbs off my underwear.

When the pads of his fingers dig into my ass cheeks I instinctively wrap my legs around his waist and am pleasantly surprised to notice that somewhere along the way he got rid of his jeans and managed to slip on a condom.

A moan escapes my throat when he backs us against the floor-to-ceiling window of our suite and his hand slips between our bodies to rub circles on my clit.

"Please," I beg. "Make me come."

He finally gives me what I want and enters me; it's like my body was starving before now. My head pushes back against the cool glass as my back arches and my nails dig into the back of his shoulders while he pounds into me. I don't think I could get any closer to this man right now even if I tried. He places a hand on the glass above my head to steady himself as he picks up his pace and really starts fucking me, like he's trying to make me forget about the last few months.

So, I oblige him and allow myself to get lost in him, in the way he feels inside of me, the warmth of his skin against mine, the feel of his mouth on my breast, moving back up to my neck and then getting lost in his kiss.

When my body detonates, he wraps his arms around me and carries me back to the bed where he lays me down gently then continues to move inside of me until I feel him stiffen with his own release. Our breaths are heavy and labored as we stare at each other, green eyes into amber ones. My eyes shut when he places small kisses on my forehead, each of my lids, the side of my mouth, and then his lips meet mine in another heated kiss before he moves off me and disposes of the condom.

When he comes back, he opens his arms for me and I snuggle into his side. We don't talk again for the rest of the night, preferring to savor everything that happened between us tonight. I wouldn't trade this moment of being held in his arms for anything in the world. It just took me a while to get to this place.

He and I spend the rest of the weekend just like we did the first night. We allow ourselves to get lost in each other because neither one of us knows what will happen when we go home and back to reality. We don't know what awaits us once we leave our cocoon.

Honestly, despite all of that, if he asked me right here right now to give us a chance, I would say yes in a heartbeat. I came so close over the last several months to losing him. That dose of reality made me realize that I don't want to waste another minute not being his. I don't want to waste another minute of not being in his arms, not hearing him say my name, of not hearing him groan when he's coming inside me.

"I can hear you thinking from over here," he teases next to me.

"Well, you need to get your super hearing checked, 'cause I

wasn't thinking anything."

The sheets rustle as his body towers over mine. "Liar," he grins.

"I am not lying."

He raises an eyebrow and it takes everything I have to keep a straight face and not give in to the fit of giggles I can feel working its way up. We lay there staring at each other for a few more seconds before his face breaks out in a smile.

"I love you."

My eyes round at the words that just left his lips. It's not the first time he's said that to me, but I thought that hearing those three words from him again would ramp up my anxiety. Turns out, I was wrong. His eyes dart to my mouth as a slow grin forms.

"I love you, too."

The giggles I was holding back escape when I get a good look at his face. It's a mixture of shock and relief. Shock that I'm not fighting him on it anymore. Relief because I said it back.

His lips crush mine in the sweetest kiss we've ever shared before he pulls back, brushing a strand of hair from my face. He's gorgeous all the time, but right now, laying naked on top of me with the moonlight streaming in and snow gently falling outside our window, he's beautiful.

"Say it again," he demands, his voice husky as his emerald eyes gaze into my amber ones.

"I love you, Jason Miller."

He grins, "I love you, Katherine Young."

20. IT'S OVER

Katherine

"Jay?" I call as I push open the front door to his house and remove my key from the door.

He doesn't answer.

We've been back from our weekend getaway for a couple weeks now and so far, things have been great. I felt like an idiot for having fought him on this mutual attraction for so long. During our getaway, I realized that I was really just using him, his body. I used him whenever I needed an escape, to forget about the whirlwind of events that have happened over the last several months. I became reliant on the escape his body provided.

I don't know when it all changed, maybe when David attacked me outside of the lingerie store, or when I was staring down the barrel of his gun, but I realized that I would miss our back and forth banter, I would miss the way one corner of his mouth would pull up into a half smile and his eyes would shine with mischief.

He was the one who suggested we take things slow when we got home, because of the whole David thing. I was okay with that. It was going to take me a while to get used to the fact that I don't have to keep fighting what I'm already feeling for him. I'm really excited to see how things progress with us.

"Jay?" I call again, poking my head into the kitchen when I don't see him in the living room.

I didn't see his truck out front but he almost never leaves his vehicles parked in the driveway. Unless he's not planning on being home long, he usually parks them in the garage.

Figuring that I probably beat him here, I make my way back out into the living room to hang up my jacket in the coat closet. Just as I reach the kitchen to start preparing lunch, a noise draws my attention and I spin around expecting to see him.

Instead, what greets me is the barrel of a handgun and five feet, five inches of angry female. If looks could kill, the one she's levelling at me could take out a whole army. I'm almost surprised that there isn't smoke emanating from her head right now. Almost.

Focus Katherine.

"Jane."

"So, you do know who I am?" The corner of her mouth pulls up in a smirk.

I nod. "I recognize you from David's office."

"If I didn't want to kill you right now, I'd be impressed. You only saw me for what? A split second? Maybe a little longer."

"You don't tend to forget the face of the woman straddling your boss in his office."

Okay, good. Keep her talking, Katherine. Just stall long enough for Jay to get here. He is coming.

"Oh, honey. He was my husband I could straddle him wherever I wanted." The sound of her laugh makes my skin crawl.

Think Katherine. What would Jay do?

I try to take in everything in my peripheral vision. Sink. Toaster. Coffee maker. Knife block. I'd like to think that my aim and throw would be faster than her trigger finger but it's highly unlikely.

And then I see it. Jay's junk drawer is slightly open, like he didn't bother closing it all the way.

It's like the heavens opened up and placed it right where I needed it when I needed it. Then in the next second I'm wondering why the hell does Jason have a 9mm hidden under random fliers and coupons in the junk drawer. To anyone who's not looking for it, it wouldn't be visible. Just the corner of the magazine is sticking out from under all the papers. I make a mental note to ask him about it later. If there is a later.

Please be loaded. Please be loaded.

"I told him that hiring you was a mistake. That people tend to look more closely at where a person goes missing. But the idiot just needed to toy with you for as long as he could," Jane continues, not noticing as I inch closer to the drawer. "Then he had to go fall in love with you, and get himself killed."

"David never loved me."

I'm closer to the drawer now, but if I can move even closer, even just an inch or two, it'll put the drawer behind my back and then maybe I can remove the gun without her knowing.

She scoffs and for a split second it looks like she has forgotten that she's pointing a gun directly at me and why she's here. "Please. He wouldn't shut up about you. He almost deserved what those friends of yours did to him." Her whole stance changes then. Her back straightens, her eyes go dark, and she's not just levelling the barrel of her gun at me but now it's pointed right at my head. "But he was my husband. So it's only fair that you pay with your life. An eye-for-an-eye and all that bullshit."

"I wasn't the one who killed him."

My fingers wrap around cold metal.

"I know. But that new boyfriend of yours will know what it's like to have someone he loves taken from him. I only wish he was here to see it."

Jason

"What are you doing here?" Danielle looks right at me as she and Parker stroll out of his office.

"I work here," I grin, raising a questioning eyebrow at her.

Danielle huffs crossing her arms. "I know that. I meant what are you still doing in the office. I thought you were supposed to be meeting Kat at your house."

The hairs on the back of my neck stand up at her words. Kat and I didn't have any plans to meet up today.

"We never made plans to see each other today. She said she was going to be busy job hunting all day."

Now it's her turn to raise a curious eyebrow at me as she pulls out her phone and starts scrolling through her messages. "She said she got a text from you an hour ago asking her to meet you for lunch at your place."

"I never..." I stand to pat down my pockets looking for my phone but it's not in my jeans or on my desk. I am pretty sure I had slipped it back into my pocket after getting out my car this morning.

Before I can finish that thought, Cole walks up and he looks like he's seen a ghost. "Jay," he says before clearing his throat. "We got a location on Jane's cell."

"Where is she?"

Cole looks to Parker then Danielle before back to me. "She's at your house."

"She knows you killed David. She's going after Kat," Parker guesses as I grab my jacket from the back of the chair and put it on.

"Over my dead body," I throw over my shoulder as we race to the elevators.

"Parker, don't let him do something stupid," I hear Dani plead.

I don't hear his response but seconds later I hear his booted feet behind me.

"Cole, get the teams geared up and meet us there, and see if you can locate Mike!" Parker yells just before the doors of the elevator close.

We ride down in silence and as soon as the doors open on the underground parking lot we're both hightailing it to one of the team SUV's.

"You can't kill her, Jay." He grabs on to the *oh-shit* handle while I slam the vehicle into drive and peel out of the parking lot.

"Why, because she's a woman?" I hiss.

"No. Because your ass is already being looked at for shooting David."

He braces his other hand against the dashboard as I drive like a bat out of hell trying to get to my girl in time.

"That was a clean shoot. You know that, man."

"I do, and the Inspector does too. Jay, you know it's just a bunch of technical bullshit. But you still can't kill her. We need to bring this one in."

I don't answer him because as soon as we turn the corner onto my street there is another big blacked-out SUV as well as our tactical vehicle.

"How the fuck did they beat us here?" My foot slams on the brake and I throw the SUV into park a split second before I'm bolting through the driver's side door.

"There's no movement from inside," Mike fills us in as soon we make it to the group.

And then, because this day couldn't get worse, my stomach sinks as a gunshot rings out. Every member from all three teams pull out their guns and then, as if we've choreographed this dance a million times, *which I guess we have*, we split into two teams; one goes around back while the other prepares to go in through the front door.

Two well-placed booted kicks to my front and back doors later, we're all splitting up into teams of two to clear the house. Parker and I clear the living room before heading to the kitchen. Kat is standing on the far side of the room, breathing hard, arms fully extended, her 9mm in her hands. I'm suddenly very glad that I hadn't given it back to her yet.

"You missed!" Jane chuckles from my kitchen floor, her left hand clutching her right arm. Her gun lies on the floor next to her.

I watch as Kat slowly lowers the gun and hands it off to Parker. To Jane she says, "I didn't miss. Killing you would've been too easy. You don't get a free pass out of paying for your actions. You deserve to rot in prison."

Cole and Mark check Jane's injured arm before hauling her off to the waiting paramedics.

"Are you okay?" I start checking Kat over as soon as I make my way to her. When I'm satisfied that she hasn't been harmed in any way, I wrap my arms around her.

I don't plan on ever letting her go.

"I'm okay."

I know that she's not when I feel her arms tremble as she wraps them around my waist. She may be physically okay but I can only imagine the emotional toll that today and the last six months must be having on her.

"Is it over?" Her voice sounds so small.

"It's over."

"Jay," she whispers.

"Yeah?"

"Can you just hold me for a little while longer."

"Babe, I'll hold you for as long as you need me to."

I keep my arms around her for a few more seconds before she's pushing away slightly. I cup her face in my hands. "I love you."

"I love you too, Jay," she responds, a smile tugging at her lips before her eyes narrow at me. "But um, why was my gun in your junk drawer?"

I drop my hands from her face and allow myself to get lost in her eyes for a second. "I had planned on giving it back to you after you passed your course but forgot and ended up putting it in the junk drawer instead."

"Are there any more randomly hidden firearms I should know about?"

A slow grin tugs at my mouth.

She laughs. "On second thought, I don't want to know."

I laugh, pulling her towards me again. "I put away a lot of bad guys doing my job. Most of the time those guys don't work alone. I'd rather be safe than sorry, and today I'm extremely grateful that it was there when you needed it. Baby, never doubt that I will do everything in my power to protect you."

"Have a seat, gentlemen." Inspector Porter motions for the three of us to enter his office and have a seat in front of his desk.

Nobody says anything for a while. Instead Parker, Mike, and I wait for Porter to start. Very few men have the ability to make me squirm in my seat, and Porter is one of them. I know he's about to rip us, or more specifically me, a new one for going rogue on Walker, and I should be worried about my career in the Emergency Response Team, but I did what I had to do to keep my girl safe. I wouldn't do anything differently.

"Look, you guys are the best I have in this unit and if I were in your shoes I would've done the same thing. But the higher-ups think that it paints the RCMP in a bad light. They think it makes it look like the ERT unit acts above the law, and I have to agree with them on that. You can't be tying up a CEO in some secret warehouse and torturing him."

"It was hardly torture," I scoff, remembering my years in the military.

"Regardless," Porter barks as he levels me with a death glare, "the three of you will have to toe the line from now on. I don't want to have to fire the three of you but if the powers-that-be aren't happy with your performance from now on, I will have little choice."

Porter looks pointedly at each of us and we nod our acknowledgement of his warning, however reluctantly.

"Good. Now, go do whatever it is you guys get up to on a free Friday night."

Brandt's is packed with its usual after work crowd when we step through the doors of the pub and the Hostess leads us towards a booth in the back. Parker orders a couple pitchers of the house brew as Cole and Mark join us.

"You think Porter will make good on his threat?" Mike asks.

"I don't doubt it. His hands are tied," Parker responds.

"What if we just started our own company," I throw out.

It's an idea that's been bouncing around in my head for a while now. With my military training and our combined years in law enforcement, it would be doable. By branching away from the RCMP and the Emergency Response Teams, it would allow us more freedom and discretion in determining which cases we want to take on. Plus, it'll allow Parker to be home with Dani and the kids whenever he needs to.

"What, like private security?" Cole asks.

I nod, taking a couple drinks of my beer. "We'd have full discretion about what cases we take on. We could, essentially, make our own hours." I look to Parker. "And you wouldn't have to leave Dani and Bella on a moment's notice."

"What would we call ourselves?" Mark ponders.

"The Protectors," Parker suggests after finishing his second beer.

"The Championers," Mike adds.

"Dude, is that even a word?" Cole laughs.

"The Guardians."

Conversation around the table stops as what I said sinks in. I look around the table at the men who have had my back since the very first day of RCMP training in Regina, and who did not think twice about helping me deal with Walker and making sure that Kat is safe. I know that I couldn't have asked for a better brotherhood than this one. One by one, each of them nods his head in agreement.

The situation with Walker brought out something in me that I never knew existed. It was completely out of character for a guy who served his country, and who was one of the best members serving in the RCMP under Porter. I acted without thought and without regard to what the consequences would be. I acted outside of the law that we're supposed to be upholding. But when someone threatens the person you love more than life, more than yourself, you'll go to any lengths to make sure they are safe and can never be harmed again.

Could I have handled it all differently? Yes, I could've, but the caveman in me had only one thing on his mind. Protect what's his, and that's what I did. I don't regret a second of it. Katherine is the reason why I'm able to keep going after seeing the things I saw while on deployment. Before meeting her, the nightmares were becoming unbearable, but now, sleep is an actual thing. I no longer wake up in night sweats, and when a nightmare does manage to squeeze its way in, just feeling her soft body curled into mine is enough for me to push the memory away.

She is a piece of me that I will always fight to protect.

Epilogue
Katherine

~One year later~

The thing about love is that you don't get to choose who you fall in love with or when you fall in love. Most of the time you never see it coming.

Then there are those times when you see it coming, and even though you try everything in your power to prevent it from happening it still smacks into you like a semi-truck. Just like the way I fell in love with Jason. He's my best friend. My protector. My fiancé.

This last year I learned that sometimes the person you don't want to love because it scares the crap out of you with just how right it feels, is the one you end up falling for the most.

And I fell hard.

I thank God every day that Jay never gave up on his love for me.

ALWAYS YOU

ABOUT THE BOOK

ALICE

Eric Knight. He was my best friend from that first day he threw sand in my hair when we were three. We were inseparable after that, there were no secrets between us, we never had to pretend with each other. Until the day in our sophomore year of high school, when he told me that he was leaving the next morning to go live with his dad on the other side of the country. He promised that once he was eighteen he would come back for me.

Three years.

For three years, I waited for him to come to back to me once he turned eighteen. He never did.

Now, fifteen years after he left, he's standing on my doorstep. He doesn't look anything like the boy who left all those years ago. He's taller, bigger, tattooed.

Scarier.

Sexier.

His chocolate-brown eyes still do to me at thirty, what they did to me at fifteen.

ERIC

Alice Johnson. I fell in love with her when we were kids. I hated turning my back on her and leaving her in our sophomore year of high school, but my mother was a stupid junkie and the court decided it would be in my best interest to live with a father I had never met. Turns out my father was the president of an MC.

I've been stuck in that life for the last fifteen years. I wanted out, and I wanted her back. But what I was about to do could get us both killed. Nobody went up against my dad and lived to tell about it.

Enough was enough. I had waited a long time to go get my girl and I am not waiting any longer. She is mine.

She has always been mine.

PROLOGUE

Just as I'm about to take the first sip of my freshly brewed coffee, the doorbell to my small one-level house rings. My brows immediately furrow together as I double check the time on my phone. Kat and Dani were early. We had made plans to do a coffee tour of all the coffee shops in town for my birthday. In Oceanview, there are about nine coffee shops and they all gave you free coffee on the day of your birthday. We figured if I went in to all of them, I could get us each three free coffees today. The plan was to break up the insane amount of caffeine with a lunch trip to Mekong for free Chinese food, then hitting up one of the Irish pubs downtown for a free dinner. I was thirty and ready to get my caffeine on before getting my drink on.

But when I open my front door, there isn't a five-foot-two, dark haired, emerald eyed female nor a five-foot-six brunette with amber eyes staring back at me. Instead, my gaze drifts up the six-foot-two frame of a very male body until it connects with his own chocolate-brown eyes. Jet black hair falls down his forehead and over one eye. His features have a ruggedness to them that wasn't there before, and he is taller than I remember. He might not be model perfect, but he always made my knees go weak, and those eyes I would recognize anywhere, even though they are haunted now. It's been fifteen years since I saw this man but the sight of him still does to me now what it did to me then. Only now, he is older and sexier. After all these years, my body remembers and still reacts to Eric Knight, maybe more so to this darker version.

His lips pull up in a small grin. "You don't remember me, do you?"

"Eric?" My voice is barely above a whisper.

He straightens up, pushing the wall he was leaning on and takes a couple steps towards me. Eric leans down, cupping the back of my head in his hand and brushes his lips over mine. And just like that I'm transported back to where it all started...

CHAPTER ONE
January 6, 1995

I'm pulling at the neckline of my dress for what feels like the hundredth time. It's my sixth birthday and my mother has insisted on putting me in another dress with three-quarter sleeves. I hate dresses and I hate the stockings that I have to wear when I wear a dress.

"Mom," I whine for the tenth time, "Can I please wear my favorite pants and sweater?" The red and black plaid skinny pants and white mickey mouse sweater is the outfit I've been living in for the past little while, much to my mother's disappointment.

"No, Alice. It's your birthday. You can wear the dress. Now, please go sit on the couch and do not get it dirty," she calls from the kitchen.

"Fine," I huff crossing my arms and spinning in my fancy Sunday-shoes towards the red sectional in our living room.

It's not long until our house is filled with aunts, uncles, cousins, and my school friends, but I'm slightly grateful that the one person I was looking forward to having come isn't here yet. I don't want him to see me in this silly dress. Hopefully, I can still convince my mom to let me change before he gets here.

But then I see his older brother walking through our front door and Eric trailing behind him.

"Happy birthday, Alice," his brother greets me and then nudges Eric with his elbow.

"Thank you, Brad."

Brad is ten years older and is usually tasked with watching Eric and I when I go over to their house for a play date. But him watching us is more like Eric and I playing in the backyard or in the basement while Brad plays video games or watches TV in the living room.

"Happy birthday, A," Eric pushes his glasses higher up on his nose and hands me a small gift wrapped box.

"Thank you, Eric," a blush creeps up my face when I remember that I'm standing in front of him wearing a dress.

"Brad. Eric," my mother's voice sounds from behind me. "Is your mom here?"

"No, she had to work, Mrs. Johnson," Brad says dropping his head and looking over at Eric, "I'm just supposed to drop Eric off. I'm going to a movie with some friends."

While Brad's talking to my mom, my eyes land on Eric but his head is downcast and he's avoiding my gaze. Eric had told me a couple days ago that their mom had lost her job again and that he was scared because she started drinking more. He didn't want to have to move across the country and live with their dad. But he said that Brad told him that would never happen, they wouldn't be going anywhere.

"Well, that's too bad. Alice, why don't you and Eric go join your cousins and your other friends in the basement."

"Okay mom," spinning on the balls of my feet I lead us to the top of the stairs where the sounds of laughter and kids playing are floating up from downstairs.

"Open your present," Eric whispers in my ear before we make our descent.

He didn't need to tell me twice. I loved opening presents. I would often ask my parents if I could open their Christmas presents for them because I loved it that much. My small hands rip at the wrapping paper until it falls away and I'm left with a small plain white box.

I look questionably over at Eric but he doesn't give anything away so I hurriedly open the box, and when I tip it upside down a small plastic police badge falls out. My eyes light up at the sight of it. Our favorite game to play together is cops and robbers. Eric and I loved it so much that we decided to make me a pretend police wallet with a paper badge in it and the id card and everything.

"Now you have an actual badge for your wallet, A. Just like the movies," he grins.

"Just like the movies," I repeat smiling.

CHAPTER TWO
January 2001

"Brad's leaving in five months," Eric says solemnly as we drag our sleds back up the snowy hill next to his house.

It's been snowing for almost the whole week, which is weird for Oceanview. We're in the valley, it normally hardly ever snows here. Needless to say, Eric and I are making the most of it and fished our sleds out of my dad's garage first thing this morning. Dad wasn't too happy that we woke him up early on a Saturday morning though.

"Where's he going?"

"College in Vancouver. I don't remember the name but I heard him talking to mom."

"He's going to college?"

Eric nods, "He got a full scholarship. Whatever that means. Him and his friends are going down at the beginning of the summer to find an apartment and get used to the city before school starts in September."

"Huh, that's cool," I move my sled back into the perfect position to go down the hill and sit down.

"Yeah, I guess," Eric says wiping the fog from his glasses before sitting down on his own sled.

We race each other down the hill a few more times before we're bored and decide to make a snowman, which turns into an ultimate snow ball fight. Eric throws his last one and it lands perfectly in the hood of my snow suit jacket. Before I can get it out he runs up to me and pulls my hood up and over my head.

Cold. So cold.

"Eric!" when I get my hood off and the majority of the snow out of my hair I turn to face him but he's doubled over laughing. His face red from the cold.

"Meanie!" I stick my tongue out at him but that just causes him to laugh harder.

"You should've seen your face," he manages to get out between bursts of laughter.

My brows knit together as I crouch down and gather up some snow in between my gloves. As soon as he sees what I'm doing, his laughter stops almost immediately and his hands shoot up in front of him while he backs away slowly. Once I'm satisfied with the amount of snow I've gathered up I stand and start forming it into a perfect circle.

"Alice…" he says still backing away.

When I look over at him with an eyebrow raised he turns and dashes for the nearest tree. Laughing, I take off after him until a snowball lands right in the middle of my jacket causing me to drop the one in my hand. Eric is laughing so hard again, he's giving away his hiding spot.

Our snowball war continues until the sun starts setting behind the houses on our street. The rule in my house is that I can stay out as long as I want if I'm on our street but because I'm only twelve I have to start making my way home as soon as the sun starts setting. It's also around the time that my mom usually has dinner ready.

Eric and I walk back over to the hill to get our sleds before making our way out of the park and towards his house.

"I don't want him to go away, A," Eric confides when his front yard comes into view.

"He'll be back for holidays, E," I try to reassure him.

"I know," he sighs looking dreadfully up his front walk way to his house.

My heart breaks for him because when his older brother leaves, Eric will be on his own. Sure, his mom would still technically be there but she hasn't taken care of him in a long time. It's Brad who makes sure Eric has a bath and that he has clean clothes for school. It's Brad who makes sure that Eric has something to eat and that his homework is done. Which makes me wonder what made him decide to go to school four hours away in Vancouver.

"I'll see ya at school on Monday, E," I say starting to make my way down the street to my house.

"Give me back my glasses, Gary."

Eric's voice carries out from the lunch room and into the hall way. I hate Gary. He's always picking on Eric, making fun of him for wearing glasses and calling him four eyes. It makes me mad that him and his friends are constantly teasing and bullying Eric for it. What I hate even more than that is when I walk into the lunch room and the rest of our grade is joining Gary in his bullying. No one is standing up for Eric.

But I will.

"Give it back to him, Gary," I march right up to him and put my hands on my hips.

"Oooo, is your girlfriend standing up for you?" Gary sing songs.

My lips pull up in a smirk. The thought of kicking him where the sun don't shine pops into my head for a split second before I shake it off.

"I'm not his girlfriend. And you're a bully," Gary's eyes go wide when I poke my finger hard into his chest. Everyone always underestimates my strength. I may be small for my age but I'm strong.

"Let's go Alice. He's not worth it," Eric tugs on my arm leading me away from Gary.

"Yeah! Run and hide behind your little girlfriend, four eyes!" Gary hollers behind us.

"Alice," Eric warns when I stop dead in my tracks. "Don't do it," he shakes his head slightly.

"What? I'm not going to do anything," I shrug my shoulders and slowly walk backwards towards Gary and his group of followers.

Eric sighs and drops his head but doesn't try to stop me.

"What? Came back for more?" Gary raises an eyebrow, tipping his soda up to his mouth.

"No, I just remembered that you had a hard time reaching that really high note in music class this morning and thought I would give you some advice," I say as innocently as I can manage.

"Yeah? What's that?" he wipes his mouth on the inside of his sleeve.

"This," my right foot swings and hits its target. A really high pitched squeal leaves his mouth as his hands fly down to cover the front of his pants and he doubles over in pain.

"See, there you go. That's what the note should sound like," I spin on my heels, much to the shock of his little group, and make my way back over to Eric. I know I'm going to pay for that later with a phone call to my parents, but I didn't care. Someone had to stand up to Gary and I didn't see anybody else brave enough to do it.

Cowards.

Nobody messes with my best friend. Maybe that wasn't the greatest way to go about dealing with Gary and his group of followers but I'm twelve. I'm not supposed to think before I act yet.

"You didn't need to do that," Eric turns to face me as soon we exit the door to the outside basketball nets. "I could've handled it."

"I know but that's what best friends are for," I lift my shoulders.

"The principal will probably call your parents."

"I know," I lower my shoulders slipping my hands into the warmth of my jacket pockets.

"Thank you," he slides his glasses back up his nose with a finger, a slow smile pulling at the corners of his mouth.

"She did what?!" my dad's voice carries through to the living room from his office and I cringe.

Guess the school principal finally called him.

Now it's just a waiting game until I'm called in to dad's office or he comes marching through that door.

One.

Two.

"Alice!" his baritone voice booms through the house.

Yup, called it.

"What's going on Neil?" my mom looks concerned as she walks in behind my dad.

"Alice apparently kicked some poor kid in the balls at lunch today."

Hearing my dad just say it out right, without beating around the bush, makes me almost laugh out loud. Almost. I'm not that stupid...or brave.

"Alice!" my mom scolds but she's not trying very hard to hide the amused smirk on her face.

"He was a bully dad! He kept teasing Eric about his glasses," I huff crossing my arms over my body. "And plus, he was having issues reaching a pitch in music class so I was just giving him some pointers."

My mom snorts and her smirk is now threatening to turn into a full-blown grin.

"Alice," my dad warns.

"Fine, I'm sorry."

"It's not me you should be apologizing to."

Our house phone rings and mom turns on her heels to go answer it. I'm pretty sure the laugh that was threatening to spill out gets let out. Dad eyes her leaving before turning back to me. A huge grin on his face.

"This never leaves this room and your mother never hears of this understand?"

I nod.

"Well done, Alice," dad laughs.

My cheeks hurt from the huge smile on my face.

"So, did he reach the correct pitch?" dad chuckles. One of the things I love about my parents is that they have no tolerance for bullies and they've always taught me to stand up for myself and my friends.

"He sure did."

Dad chuckles some more before his face goes serious again. "Alice, I know that we taught you to stand up for yourself and for anyone who's being bullied. And I'm extremely proud of you for doing that. But, kicking someone there isn't *always* the answer. You get that right?"

I nod, "I know dad. But Gary deserved it. It's not just Eric he bully's. And he gets away with it too! None of the teachers care that he's doing what he's doing. I was tired of it."

"Why do you think that the teachers don't care?"

I look tentatively up at my dad, "because I've told them about what he does and they haven't done anything about it."

My dad looks like he's lost in thought then he turns back to me, ruffling my hair. "I'll look into it, Kiddo. But promise me you won't be going around kicking any more boys."

He's on the school board so I know that when he says he'll look into it I can guarantee that he will. "I promise."

"Good. Now go help your mom with dinner."

PLAYLIST

"You and Tequila" by Kenny Chesney

"Nothin' Like You" by Dan and Shay

"Kiss Me" by Ed Sheeran

"Concrete Angel" by Martina McBride

"Red Dress" by Jojo Mason

"Little Toy Guns" by Carrie Underwood

"Just A Fool" by Christina Aguilera

"Starving" by Hailee Steinfeld

"My Way" by Calvin Harris

"Let Me Love You" by Mario

"Time" by Dean Brody

"We Are One" by 12 Stones

"One Call Away" by Charlie Puth

"Body Like a Back Road" by Sam Hunt

"All Of Me" by John Legend

"Like I'm Gonna Lose You" by Meghan Trainor ft. John Legend

"All The Way" by Jacob Bryant

ACKNOWLEDGEMENTS

To my husband, J, thank you for putting up with me during the writing process, and supporting me in this crazy dream.

To my brother, M, and my mom, words cannot describe how grateful I am for your encouragement and your support. I love you.

JM Walker at Just Write. Creations, you did an amazing job on this cover. Thank you.

Laura Hull, Red Pen Princess (Indies Ink), thank you for taking on this project on such short notice. You're amazing!

Teolia Mitchell. There are no words to describe how thankful I am for you and your support. There were days when I didn't think I would be able to continue on this journey, but your messages kept me going. Thank you! Thank you! Thank you! I hope I get to meet you at a future signing :)

My Alpha, Beta, and ARC readers. I'm thankful for each and every one of you. Your support and encouragement are what keeps me writing.

To the readers who stuck with me and read *Piece of Me* from beginning to end, thank you. I hope you enjoyed the ride, and I can't wait for you to read Alice and Eric's story in *Always You*.

About the Author

You can take the girl out of the ocean but you cannot take the ocean out of the girl. A.J believes that describes her to a T. She practically grew up on a beach in Cape Town, South Africa until her family immigrated to Canada. However, the ocean still has a way of relaxing her. If she can't get to the water, then a long drive with the music blaring will work just fine.

She wears her heart on her sleeve and is a self-proclaimed hopeless romantic who believes that everyone deserves their happily ever after. A.J. lives in BC, Canada with her husband. When she's not writing, she's reading. She loves the NFL and drinks way too much coffee.

If you enjoyed reading *Piece of Me*, please leave a review on your favorite book retailer and/or Goodreads.

Other books by the author

Behind These Eyes series:
Skin Deep (January 2017)
Piece of Me (June 2017)
Always You (September 2017)

The Guardians series (Spinoff from Behind These Eyes series):
Brad (February 2018)
Cole (July 2018)

Standalones:
Un•breakable (2018)

Contact A.J.:

EMAIL: a.daniels.author@gmail.com
FACEBOOK: A.J. Daniels Author
INSTAGRAM: A.J_Daniels_Author
TWITTER: @AJDanielsAuthor

www.ingramcontent.com/pod-product-compliance
Lightning Source LLC
Chambersburg PA
CBHW030252130626
46549CB00002B/501